BLOOD IN THE FORUM

MARIUS SCROLLS
BOOK TWO

VINCENT B. DAVIS II

THIRTEENTH PRESS LLC

Dedicated to Edie and DiAnn. I'm so thankful that God placed both of you in my life.

READING ORDER

A WORD FROM SERTORIUS

If anyone were to ask me, in my old age and as I continue to fight against my own countrymen, when the death of the Republic began, I would point to the tribuneship of Tiberius Gracchus.

I'm certain that this is subjective, and many others would direct you to another event as the root cause of Rome's decay, but I believe the life and death of Tiberius Gracchus has always stood parallel to the life and death of the Roman Republic as I understand it.

There is no event in all the annals of Rome's history spoken about more infrequently, or more quietly. For decades now the name of Tiberius Gracchus has hardly been uttered above a whisper, and it's easy to understand why. Even in a city littered with corpses, surrounded by marble temples and colonnades splattered with blood, the very name of the infamous Tribune still elicits shutters. He was the one who started it all. And for some this has meant glory, power, and wealth. For others, the precedents he set have caused agony, poverty, famine, and death.

So, it was a surprise when General Marius wrote up his

own experience of those turbulent years so long ago and freely shared it with me.

I'm certain that if these scrolls here contained had ended up in the wrong hands, the general's meteoric rise to power would have been halted. Even the great Marius might have found his corpse numbered amongst the countless hordes of Gracchan sympathizers who washed up, bloated and bloodless, on the banks of the river Tiber.

But the men in power can do no more harm to the general's name or legacy, or to my own. Marius asked that I keep this private, but I don't think he would mind now, considering he's long dead.

It is more important that the world know the truth about Rome, and how she's become the corrupt gorgon she is. You will here witness the life and death of Tiberius Gracchus, and decide for yourself whether he was a great man, or a demagogue, as his enemies claimed him.

PART I

ribune Sertorius,

OR SHOULD I be calling you citizen Sertorius now? I guess
we aren't back into the city yet, but we will be soon. And
then you'll have to take off your crest. What will you do
then, I wonder? Who will you be? The options are endless,
young man, but I have an intuition. I believe you'll follow
down the path of your general, and wade into the world of
politics. It is what one witty fellow called "the sewers of
Romulus". That may be true, but politics, I think, is where
you belong. And I am always correct in my assessment of
the men under my command.

I wrote this little piece in boredom. We're sitting here,
waiting outside of Rome's gates, for the glory I've earned.
And it called to mind a time when I was forced to do the
same thing under the command of my general, Scipio
Aemilianus, whom I told you about previously.

To be honest, I'm quite proud of this writing. I considered posting it on the steps of the Capitol. This would show those arrogant aristocrats that I'm a bit more than just a soldier. I can't do that, though. To even whisper the name of Tiberius Gracchus is to invite doom on your life. If the suggestion was made that I ever sympathized with the man, I'm afraid the support of the people and the entire army standing behind me wouldn't be enough to protect me from the nobles. For that reason, I'd ask that you keep this to yourself.

But, if you'll allow me to give myself some credit, I believe that last letter I wrote had some impact on you. During our campaign against the Cimbri, you transformed from a dark, morose man into a true warrior. And I trust that my writing to you played some role in that change. For that reason, and because I believe your next step as a Roman is to enter public life, I'll share my first experience foraying in the political arena.

I hope this will guide you as my commands have in battle.

THE ROMAN TRIUMPH is a glorious thing. Glorious doesn't begin to describe it. Rapturous? Not that even. I await, with joy, the idea of you and all the rest of our soldiers experiencing it for the first time, as soon as the Senate stops their groveling and gives us a date.

During a Triumph, Rome is as it should be. It's how one should always imagine it. The entire city, teeming with life. Men, women and children, bustling on every street and bursting from the seams of every back alley. They climbed statues and hung from rafters, they leaned out of windows and stood on the rooftops.

And each one cheered.

Applause louder than the war cries we had so recently experienced, loud enough to almost drown out the echo in our minds. Flower petals rained down on us like a blizzard in the Gallic hills. They say the triumphant general is a god for that day, but I say we all were. Every man was anxious to shake your hand, every woman a willing participant in service to the city.

And despite all this, Scipio's triumph was quite meager compared to others. There was essentially no war booty to return with. The Numantines were wretched creatures by the time we conquered them, and what little of wealth they once possessed has been burned to keep themselves warm during that long siege. For that reason, the entire Triumph was paid for from the pocket of Scipio Aemilianus himself. Some might call that a wasted expenditure, but he'd have been damned if he returned to anything other than to adoring applause after all we had endured.

Poor man, he even had to pay us legionaries from his own pocket, something that would have been absurd to those skinflint senators who had never wielded a sword. Each man received six sesterces for the day. A remarkably low sum, to be certain, but we knew the general had paid for it himself. He refused to allow our service to go unrecognized, and we loved him all the more for it.

I marched with the tribunes a few paces behind Scipio's chariot. Despite the adoring applause and the showers of rose petals, he remained fixed, as if etched in stone, with his back straight and head forward, one arm raised to the sky to greet his citizens.

I felt he truly was a god on that day. He was everything a Roman should hope to be, and more. I longed, deeply, in my soul, to be like him one day, although I never expected another Roman to fill his sandals, at least not in my lifetime.

"You think it will go to his head?" a fellow soldier, and longtime acquaintance Rutilius Rufus shouted over the cheers.

"He deserves it. He's a god after all," I said, nodding at a pretty girl with waterfall curls, as she reached across the partition to touch my arm.

"For one day only."

When we came to a halt, Scipio took his place before the procession, and remained silent while the king of the Numantines was brought before him. Ropes had previously been secured around the conquered king's neck, and at the flick of Scipio's wrist, the carnifex pulled a lever. The rope instantly tightened and hoisted the king a few inches off the ground. The crowd fell silent, a strange sort of reverence, as the king gasped silently.

As the king's legs quit flailing, and his body fell limp, Scipio lowered his head, as if he too had been strangled.

After a moment of silence, Scipio raised his head once more, to the rapturous applause of the entire populace of Rome, twice as loud as it had been previously.

AFTER THE SACRIFICES WERE MADE, the triumph was concluded. The soldiers were released and given liberty to celebrate in whatever ways they saw fit, but the other officers and I lingered nearby for a while. Scipio had much more important matters to attend to, but we couldn't leave without a goodbye. Most wished for the great man to remember them as they planned to run for political office, or they required some favor or another.

I couldn't leave for other reasons however. Scipio had told me when to shit, bathe, and shave for so long, I hardly knew what to do with myself without receiving an order. Where was I supposed to go? What was I to do now? I couldn't return to Arpinum now, even if I had wanted to. After all I had seen during that campaign, I would have killed myself from boredom. As ludicrous as it sounds, I hoped that if I remained with Scipio long enough, he might just have another order for me.

I also wanted to remain near the great man for as long as possible. I had no favors to ask, but wanted to bask in his glory. I wanted to see how he addressed his people, how he shook the hands of those senators who approached him as if he were king.

"Sir, it has been a pleasure and an honor serving under you," I said when it was at last my turn to address him.

He took a moment to appraise me before replying. His face was painted scarlet like the war-god he was impersonating, and his gaze was sharp as he analyzed.

"Where's your little girl?" he asked. I stammered for a moment but he smiled, "Yes, I've heard. Where is she?"

"I left her with my cousin. She has a farm north of the Via Latina. I was planning to go get here when I'm dismissed... now that I'm dismissed I mean," I said, terribly embarrassed.

He placed a hand on my shoulder and bade me to meet his gaze.

"She has waited a while. She can wait a little longer. You should join me for dinner tonight," he said, turning to nod to the next man who wished to steal a moment of his time.

"With you, sir?" I didn't believe what I was hearing. I

replayed his words a few times in my head, cautious that I hadn't misinterpreted.

"Yes, dinner. With me."

"Is that allowed, sir?" I stammered like an imbecile.

"You're not a tribune anymore. And I'm not a general. We're both citizens now."

"No... I meant... our classes..." I said. He was a patrician and I wasn't. I'm not sure why I objected in the first place, except that I didn't believe I was truly deserving of this offer.

"You're an equestrian aren't you?" he asked. I nodded in the affirmative. "Well then, it's perfectly appropriate. Besides, my in-laws will be attending, and they're plebeian, so I assume anyone can come." He laughed sardonically. I tried to reply, but no words came out. I assume my face looked rather perplexed, as he continued, "I need someone tough with me because I'm afraid my brother by law might poison me.

My eyes flew open as he burst into a laugh.

"Gaius? The tribune from Spain? He would never hurt you?" I said, stunned. The general's wife had a brother who served with us in Spain, Gaius Gracchus, and he had seemed very pedestrian in my appraisal, a young man simply seeking to serve his time and honor the tradition of his forebears.

He patted my face, "I meant his brother Tiberius, but I spoke in jest. Stand by for just a moment while I address your comrades, and then we will convene at my Domus."

He turned to speak with the others, who I took note did not receive the same offer I did. All the while, I practiced my posture and stance, and recited the lines I might be required to say in the presence of Rome's elite.

AFTER SCIPIO HAD CONCLUDED with his well-wishers and sycophants he led me back to his Domus on the Capitoline. The place was so damned big, I would have gotten lost in it had a slave not led me by the arm to the baths.

Steam was rising from the waters like a burning city, and for a moment I was almost afraid to step in, until the young girl—probably a Greek of about twenty years and with beautiful black hair down to her ass—stepped into the waters and beckoned me to come forth. I hesitated for a moment before I took off my sword belt and pulled the tunic over my head. The rest was a bit of a dream, as the exhaustion of the past years and the warmth blended to cause me to sleep. The slave girl poured lavender on her hands and massaged my shoulders and poured water over my head from a clay vase. I hadn't yet taken wine that evening, but I'll tell you, I was intoxicated. I've never taken a bath quite like that since.

When I was finished, three other slaves wrapped me in one of Scipio's togas, which surprisingly fit very well. It was finely pressed and scented, seemingly never worn. The thread was so soft, yet so heavy, it seemed to caress the skin. All this pampering made a provincial like myself a bit uncomfortable, as I'm sure it would make you, but I'll admit I loved it. I wanted more of it. I desired it.

I waited in the atrium for Scipio to finish his own preparations for the evening, and I admired the death masks on the walls, each one passed down from the consuls in Scipio's lineage. How many great men could come from one family? It stunned me more than the warmth of the baths, the fine threads of the togas, or the beautiful lilies of Scipio's *peristylium*. Candles flickered behind each one and illuminated their eyes. Their brows were poised and their lips were slightly opened, as if they wanted to say something, as if they wanted to tell me their story.

I followed the masks from the first until the last, and ran my fingers over the warm edges of the mask. His features defined and noble, he must have been a young man when he died, but what a legacy he had left behind! What must it be like to be the patron of such a family? The first Scipio must have been welcomed on Mount Olympus for ushering in a people who led Rome through politics and war for so many generations.

"Ah, you've met Maluganensis," Scipio said, startling me. He had a coy smile on his face as he approached, adjusting his wrist plates.

"I tried to ask his name but he wouldn't tell me," I replied, my best attempt at humor.

"He was the first Scipio." He spoke with a reverence usually reserved for the gods. "And each man in my line has sought to top him. He was the Master of the Horse to Camilius, you know? I'm not sure if I'll ever surpass that, no matter how many empires I topple." Scipio grew quiet, and I returned my attention to the men who watched silently from the halls of Scipio's Domus.

"You're imagining what your face would look like in one of those, aren't you?" Scipio says. As I turned to him again, I expected there to be humor in his eyes, but there was none. "No, you're imagining what it would be like to have so many masks following you." He nodded as if he understood.

Before I formulated a response, he slapped me on the shoulder. "Come on, then. I'll show you glory in modern politics isn't quite as impressive as our forebears would leave us to believe."

WE WAITED OUTSIDE for an extended moment, beside Scipio's lictors and two litters flanked by hefty Carthaginian slaves.

"If my wife is planning to meet her friends for an afternoon of weaving she's as punctual as a priest. But if I ask her to attend a dinner with me, well, she takes her time," Scipio said, impatiently tapping his foot.

When the door opened, from it stepped Scipio's wife, Sempronia. Perhaps it was because she was the first noble lady I had seen up close, but I was stunned by her beauty. She had plump lips and thin eyebrows, soft skin powdered by her servants to perfection. I would have been too paralyzed to speak if she had addressed me, but fortunately she didn't. She passed by her husband and me both, pausing only to allow Scipio to offer her a lift onto the litter. Patricians are often strange about showing affection in public, but I was still a bit surprised, as this was likely the first time they had seen each other for over a year.

After she reclined inside the litter, the slaves carried it off, and Scipio climbed into the one behind it. I walked beside him.

"I spoke in jest about them poisoning my wine," Scipio said through the sheer partition between us, "but they will try to pour poison in your ear." He turned away from me and said, almost to himself, "their politics are not mine."

As we walked, I noticed a great deal of graffiti lining the walls of Rome's streets. One of them in particular was the crude drawing of a man, brandishing a large erect phallus pissing on the drawings of several poor senators. Above the offender was the name TIB GRACCHVS. I didn't know much about the politics of Scipio's brother-in-law, but that told me about all I needed to know.

When we arrived at the location of our dinner party, I was surprised to find the home of Scipio's mother-in-law to be much larger than Scipio's. Despite the size, the doors were gilded, the wolf's heads on each made of fine silver. It was easy to see that the Domus was ancient, perhaps as old as the first mask on Scipio's wall. There was something respectable about a family that remains within the confines of its ancestral grounds.

"Make way for the Proconsul Publius Cornelius Scipio Aemilianus, Imperator of the Spanish legions, conqueror of Numantine and Carthage!" Scipio's lictor shouted through the front door, neglecting to use the door rings placed within the wolves' mouths like a normal guest might.

"Really, Flavius, that is a bit hostile for a dinner party," Scipio said irritably as he helped his wife from their litter. Sempronia wrapped her arm around his, a proper husband and wife, but they noticeably kept their gazes far apart.

As we entered, a noble lady approached.

"You've returned to us at last," she said, kissing Scipio on both cheeks before embracing her daughter. I'm certain there were tapestries adorning the walls, and marble busts from Greece spread throughout the atrium, but it was nothing compared to the woman who possessed them. I could hardly look away.

And one can hardly blame me. This woman, Scipio's mother-in-law, was the daughter of Scipio Africanus, the man who defeated Hannibal himself. She was the closest thing to a princess Rome would ever have.

She was well into her fifties at this point, but age hadn't tarnished her beauty any more than it had tarnished her father's legacy. Her hair was dark with hints of red, drawn up atop her head in carefully delineated locks, a tiara placed on top. Gold earrings dangled almost to her shoulders, and a long necklace set with sapphires clung to her pronounced bust. Elegant, yet tasteful.

"And this is one of my tribunes, Gaius Marius," Scipio said, jogging me back to the present.

"It's a pleasure, young warrior," she extended a hand, allowing me to kiss it delicately.

"The pleasure is all mine, ma'am." I considered saying something about how reading about her father's exploits had fascinated me as a boy, and made me a better soldier as a man. I decided better of it though. I'm certain she was had grown bored of such flagrant flattery.

As Cornelia led us into the triclinium, I first noticed the elegance of the mosaics adorning the floors and ceilings. Each designed by the most skilled of craftsmen by the look, they were both beautiful and somber. They told of ancient glories and ancient sorrows, and for the first time I realized that the last time I set foot within a Roman home was the rundown villa of my father. My chest tightened and my heartbeat quickened as I realized I didn't quite belong, no matter how pleasantly our host had greeted me.

I'm sure you felt something similar when you first set foot within the home of that crusty old bastard Gnaeus Caepio.

When we entered, every man and woman present stood to their feet and applauded Scipio. He smiled and waved for them to calm themselves.

There were several present whose names I do not remember, but I do recall seeing Gaius Gracchus, a young man I had grown to know a bit in Spain. In him I found a quick refuge, as I was anxious to dialogue with someone with whom I had something in common.

"Tribune Gracchus, it's good to see you again."

"Marius? Well, I didn't expect to find you hear of all places." He stood and shook my hand, clapping his other on my shoulder. I suddenly relaxed, now that I had a companion for the evening. He was a charming young lad, really. He had a mop of boyish hair, which had irritated Scipio awfully on campaign. The iris of his hazel eyes was ringed with black, his eye lashes as long and curly as a woman's. Now that I think of it, he was a touch feminine in his way, but he never shied from a fight on the battlefield, or in the forum later on.

"Our general was kind enough to invite me," I said, a bit more enthusiastically then I might have.

We hadn't much in common, or much to discuss except warfare, which seemed unpleasant for a dinner party. So, our discussion quickly devolved into awkward silence.

"Ah, this is my new wife, Licinia," he said, gesturing to a pretty young girl on the couch he had been previously reclining on.

"Greetings," she extended a hand, but didn't stand.

"We married while we were awaiting the triumph."

I accepted her hand and congratulated them both, but quickly took my leave, as there was little else either Gaius or myself could think of to continue our conversation.

Cornelia showed me to the couch I would be using that evening, but before I could recline there was another standing ovation.

Entering the dining room was the notorious Tribune of the Plebs himself, Tiberius Gracchus. The guests all cheered for him as if he were the returning conqueror. I stole a glance at Scipio, who was flushing with irritation. Everyone was standing, some clapping and others cupping their hands over the mouths to shout praises. Everyone was standing, that is, except the Proconsul himself.

He was slender, even for a young man his age, but was not without muscle. His forearms were particularly broad, and I remember them as being remarkably vascular. He had swept back and boyish hair, but it was a bit shorter and more traditional than his little brother Gaius'. He was clean shaven, so close it appeared he hadn't yet grown his first beard, and his chin was pronounced, his jawline strong. His eyes were as alert and alive as the fires of Vesta. He seemed to be chiseled from stone, prepared from the start for a statue of his own. Perhaps it was my first cup of wine already setting in, or my recent fixation with Scipio's first ancestor, but the man appeared to be a death mask come to life.

But perhaps more than anything, I remember that he was exceedingly fashionable, wearing the tunic loosely around the shoulders and waist, which was the style of the day. He was both modern and traditional in the same instance, a strange paradox, given the times and his reputation.

"You embarrass me," he said to his fans, accepting a handshake or kiss from each in their turn, lingering especially in an embrace with his mother, whom he appeared to cherish. This made the gathering cheer even more.

They all gathered around him, in such a way that made Scipio's entrance appear meager. I had heard some gossip about the radical tribune, but had kept my head buried in maps, provisioning documents, and muster calls for so long that I had hardly taken notice. Perhaps I would have inquired a touch more if I had known I would have been sharing a meal with the man so soon. But such a notion would have seemed impossible to me before the moment itself.

Tiberius nodded along as they heaped their praises upon him, but seemed distracted. Until his gaze shifted across the room, and locked with Scipio's.

Scipio slowly stood to his feet, and the two maintained fixed eye contact as the room slowly grew quiet.

Scipio's hand twitched. Tiberius' jaw flexed. For a moment I thought the cup of wine in Tiberius' hand might fall, and a fist take its place.

Just before the tension become too difficult to bear, a smile split across Tiberius' face.

"How are you, dear brother? It's been a long time," Tiberius said, embracing him. Scipio, more cautiously, eventually accepted it and patted the man's back.

"Brother by law," Scipio said, but Tiberius pretended not to hear it.

Before long, food was brought out and partitioned around the room. Thankfully, no one inquired about my presence, and I was allowed to gorge myself in relative anonymity. The only time I was mentioned was when Scipio told of how he saw me kill an enemy king in single combat. They gasped and nodded in admiration, and I lacked the courage to tell them the man I killed wasn't a king by any measure, and that has been the tradition ever since.

The wine flowed freely. It was a celebration by all accounts. Scipio told a few embellished tales of his time in Spain, and Gaius Gracchus doted over his new wife, feeding her figs and giggling as if no one else was present.

"When you left for Spain I had no notion you'd possibly return with more glory than you had after conquering Carthage," Tiberius complimented Scipio.

"I would have returned with more glory if my brother by law wasn't pandering to the peasantry at the cost of ancient tradition," Scipio replied, calmly but not without malice.

The mood of the room shifted drastically.

"Come now, it's only the wine talking," Cornelia said, but Tiberius lifted his hand to placate her. Tiberius' young wife Claudia tugged at his sleeve as if to say "leave it until tomorrow", but he replied with a nod as if to say, "it's okay, I'll handle it."

Everyone grew silent and stared at their sandals. The only person in the room who remained unaffected was the accused man himself, Tiberius.

"Dear me, I had no notion you believed such things. I had no intention of offending your aristocratic friends, brother, but I had no choice! Your friend, the good former Consul Laelius tried to pass similar legislation at the start of his term, but was shut down by the Senate immediately. Then, he tucked tail and ran. I knew if I wanted to pass my bill, I had no choice but to avoid approaching the Senate," he replied, not seeming offended in the least. Scipio sipped his wine and watched Tiberius, as if waiting for him to crack. "The measure needs to be passed, brother—"

"Brother by law," Scipio interjected.

"The legislation needs to be passed, and unlike your friend Laelius, I won't allow antiquated precedents or old men from good families to keep it from happening."

Scipio's wife Sempronia, the sister of the Gracchi brothers, rolled her eyes and took her leave. I began to presume this wasn't the first time such discussions had taken over a family dinner. Cornelia followed after her.

Scipio said nothing, so Tiberius continued, "These political procedures I failed to observe are bloated and outdated. A man as intelligent as yourself has to realize that the rules once meant to govern a city state have no place governing a Republic."

"And who, by Jupiter Capitolinus, gives you the right to make such judgement!" Scipio roared. For my general and his brother-in-law, it had only been the two of them in the room for some time. Now, it was quickly coming close to that, as the rest of the guests slowly poured out. Before long, it was just the three of us.

Tiberius continued unperturbed. "This legislation *needs* to be passed, and it needs to happen quickly. We don't have time for the bandying of pointless words and half measures. We need action."

I didn't understand what they were talking about, not in the slightest. But the conviction with which Tiberius spoke compelled me. I wanted to know more.

"Quickly? What you actually mean is that you need to have the measures passed by the end of your term as tribune?" Scipio asked, and now it was time for Tiberius to be silent. "Tell me, what makes you the man who has the right to change the very foundation Rome is built upon, to alter the sacred tradition?"

Tiberius stood and took a few long strides around the room. Scipio poured himself another cup of wine and waited for the retaliation as if the two were circling one another in a Greek wrestling match.

"I'm sure many men are capable. But few are willing. Easier to protect the status quo and benefit from it, while Rome's citizens starve and die around us."

"Do not insinuate that I like citizens starving. Who has done more to bring Rome vast wealth than I?" Scipio leaned forward on his couch, menace in his eyes.

"Wealth that has been hoarded by the aristocracy,"

Tiberius replied without pause. Then both men fell silent, declining to follow that conversation any further, as it might have quickly resulted in violence if they had. "I might have pissed off several of the leading men in the Senate by bypassing them and putting my measures directly before the Assembly of the People, but out of the three leading families, I have the support of two. The Claudians and Scipiones both support me, unless the latter would betray me." Scipio looked away and said nothing. I could tell he was intoxicated.

At this point, I considered standing and taking my leave. Both men had long since forgotten my presence. The only thing that kept me on my couch was the difficulty in deciding whether I would be more inconspicuous by leaving or by remaining as still as possible. That, and a keen interest in discovering what in Gaia's name these men were talking about.

Then, to my terror, Tiberius turned to me. Why was I terrified? I was afraid something in those icy eyes might compel me to join him. I feared that hypnotic gaze might force me to utter something which would repulse my mentor.

"Let's put it to him," Tiberius said gesturing to me.

"Leave him out of this," Scipio replied, looking over his shoulder and appearing to be surprised I was still there.

"Gaius Marius," Tiberius said, remarkably remembering my name from the brief, informal introduction he had received during the meal, "Gaius Marius, what do you believe Rome's greatest problem is?"

I looked to Scipio for permission to speak, but he didn't meet my gaze.

"I've been away far too long to know," I replied sheepishly.

"If you don't know, I will tell you."

"Young men and their ambition... that's Rome's greatest threat," Scipio mumbled underneath his breath.

Tiberius began to pace as he spoke, "Most of our grain comes from foreigners, such as the Sicilians. This is because all of our land has been swallowed up by the aristocracy, who no longer use our fertile fields for grain, but rather for cultivating cash crops—olives for oil and grape for wine."

"How long is this going to last?" Scipio shook his head.

"The people are going hungry because the slave uprising in Sicily has restricted the supply they can provide us with. So, it appears we will be forced into famine each time a foreign nation goes to war." Tiberius seemed to form an idea as he spoke, and he collected empty wine cups from around the room. He set one of them on the table between us.

He continued, "And those farms which do exist no longer hire Roman free men, but rather slaves. Our recent conquests, many of which were overseen by the great general before us, have resulted in such a massive influx of slaves that their prices have bottomed out. They can be purchased cheaper than an amphora of wine, if you find a good deal. So, Rome is faced with unemployment." He set another cup of wine beside the first. "The unemployed flock to the city, abandoning their ancestral farms, seeking to benefit from the grain dole of the city, which we've previously discussed are lacking because of the Sicilian war. More demand, less supply."

"Marius doesn't want to hear your tricks, Tiberius," Scipio said, but his voice wavered.

Tiberius ignored him and continued, "And since only landed men can serve in the military, and that class is dwindling because the aristocracy has gobbled up all the farms like Egyptian hippos, there are fewer and fewer men available for service. This means that those who do qualify are called upon again and again to serve, so often that they cannot maintain their farms. Which causes them to default on their taxes. Which forces them to sell their ancestral lands at bottom prices to the wealthiest bidders, creating a vicious cycle." Tiberius set another empty wine chalice beside the first two.

"To serve your country, no matter how often, is the highest honor!" Scipio said with a snarl.

"If it is such an *honor*, why do we not *honor* the men who return?" Tiberius replied.

"I think my Triumph today proves that Rome honors her veterans."

"We honor them for a day only, with the cheers of a drunken mob and liberty to drink and make love. But do we honor them with a roof over their heads?"

Scipio laughed.

"But do we? The wild beasts that roam over Italy have their caves or a den to lurk in. But the men who fight and die for Rome... what do they have? Light and air is all that's left to them. Homeless they drift here, to the city, to slowly die of starvation at the foot of our waning granaries."

"You are misinformed," Scipio said, his laughter evaporating, "to serve, you must have land. Like you previously mentioned."

Tiberius stepped closer to his brother-in-law, smiling sadly. He placed a hand on Scipio's arm and said, "You have been gone far too long, brother. When these men serve year after year, they return to their appropriated land to find it consumed by the growing acreages and latifundia of the rich. So they return homeless. Drifters and vagrants." Scipio grunted, finding nothing else to say on the matter.

Tiberius stepped away from his brother-in-law and back behind his table with the carefully placed, empty cups of wine.

"So, I propose we redistribute the public land. Give the homeless farms of their own, alleviating the homelessness in the city, which would lessen the demand of an increased grain dole." Tiberius flicked the first cup, sending to crashing into the cold mosaics beneath us. "These men would have land, so they'd be eligible to serve in the legion. And since the body from which the military is drawn would be much larger, the individual man would be required to serve less time." He pushed over the second cup. "These farms would rear grain, rather than olives or grapes. And since this grain would then be taxed, a portion of their grain would be added to our granaries, to feed those who don't receive farms." He slowly tipped over the final cup, the clatter echoing out the silent triclinium.

"You speak with fine words, Tiberius. What a display! If you'd only rally the lute players and a troupe of actors, you could put on a spectacle!"

Tiberius looked at me again, and I was afraid the look in my eyes might convey that he was swaying me. I was careful to look away. "But this proposal pisses off the rich. Why? Because it is their land which would be redistributed. Never mind the fact that the law has always stated that no man, no matter how influential or affluent, should own more than 500 iugera of public land. The law has fallen silent before the incessant wailing of the rich."

"And have you forgotten that you are one of them?" Scipio shouted and stomped his foot.

But Tiberius' grey eyes were still fixed on me. "I only wish to enforce an old law. But I cannot go through the traditional channels. If I brought my bill before the Senate,

I'd be howled down from the lowest bench to the rafters. The Senate would block my every move, because the Senate is made up of the very people who have the most to lose. The very same men who caused this whole mess to begin with."

I looked to Scipio. I hoped Tiberius had adequately swayed him, as he had swayed me, so that I could freely express myself. But he stood abruptly and held out a hand to silence his brother-in-law.

"And how will this measure be enacted? Who will take away the land from those whose father's fathers tilled that earth? You? The very man who proposes the distribution? That isn't a conflict of interests? Oh, but no. You, the great paragon of virtue, would hardly be an unfair judge."

Tiberius crossed his arms and looked away, "It's irrelevant how the measure is enacted or who is in charge of enforcing it. It simply needs to be done. Have I not proven that already?"

"And farming is hard labor. You believe those reprobate layabouts will truly wake up at dawn and till the earth for their sustenance when they've become so used to receiving handouts?"

Tiberius turned, his eyes ablaze, as rapturous as if he had just discovered the cure for leprosy.

"We should debate it!"

"Come again?" Scipio's eyes narrowed.

"We should debate, from the rostra. We will state our cases before the people." Tiberius spoke with renewed fire.

"I'm a senator, not a demagogue."

"Come now! The people love me for standing up for the rights, but you are the true people's champion. The conqueror of Numantia and Carthage? Surely they will listen to you if no one else."

"The people don't know what's best for them."

"But they would surely listen to their hero, Scipio Aemilianus. I am simply an instrument of the people. If you can sway them, I will repeal my legislation. I am a tribune, and exist only to do their will."

Scipio's eyes lit up as well. If he could defeat Tiberius in a debate, and stop this whole issue before it began, he would be a new kind of savior of Rome. Perhaps that would finally put him on equal footing with his noble ancestor Maluga-nensis. He would be a hero to the people and the aristocracy.

"When?"

"Tomorrow, certainly. The vote is in three days. If I'll be forced to repeal it, I'll need to do it soon." Even as they spoke, forgetting again that I was present, I believed Tiberius was walking Scipio into a trap. But the scent of glory had shrouded his judgement.

"We will debate then." Scipio said reluctantly, but perhaps part of his reticence was for show. Each man appeared to think he was getting the better of the other.

"Well, if that's the case, we better get to bed. No one enjoys nursing a hangover while giving a speech."

Tiberius and Scipio reluctantly shook hands. Scipio and I exited into the cool night air.

"Sometimes," he said as he stirred his slaves to their feet and climbed into his litter, "the lion must swipe at his cubs to teach them a lesson. It's never pleasant, but it's necessary. That's what is going to happen tomorrow," he said, fixing his eyes forward.

THINGS WERE DIFFERENT THEN. Now it seems like every other day is a holiday or a festival of some sort, and there is always some ambitious young Aedile who spends lavishly on entertainment in hopes that the masses will favor him for the consulship when his time comes. It wasn't so then.

And because Rome lacked constant entertainment and gratification, the citizenry flocked to debates like the one between Scipio and Tiberius. They watched, rapturous, as if they were two champions dueling it out in the arena, in reverential silence, as if they were priests reporting the auspices.

Scipio insisted I stay in his home after the dinner party. Therefore, I was there while he and his clients prepared to march to the forum together. It only made sense that I should follow him and his attendants to the heart of Rome to see my general in a different kind of arena.

The entire republic was controlled from the forum, and it was easy to tell. A provincial like me was constantly stunned by the heights of those buildings. How did the builders do it? How did the stone reach such heights without being lifted by the arm of a god?

Scipio must have noticed my awe.

"It's marvelous isn't it? It's easy to forget, when we're out on campaign for so long."

"The stone is so white... white as snow. I'll never understand how they cut it." I analyzed a column as we passed it by.

"It likely took 3,000 slaves to hack that one bit of stone there. Nothing we have has come easily. You know the forum was a swamp once? A fetid marshland swarming with mosquitos and snakes. It was impossible to build here. A single building would have sunk into the mud beneath."

"I had no idea," I said. Looking around at the stone

roads and the high arches, marble statues of Mars, every contour of his face screaming with life, it was hard to imagine.

"But we Romans have always been an industrious people. We drained the swamps, and funneled the water to the Tiber. We turned these hills into the center of Gaia's earth. And some of the world's finest men have walked these streets before us. And now..." he shook his head and analyzed the crowds waiting for him, "we are left with these."

The debate was to be held from the rostra, a platform cut from the finest stone, facing out across a vast courtyard wide and long enough to host the majority of Rome's most inquisitive citizens. The most distinguishing element, however, was the presence of a dozen or so ship beaks nailed to the front of it. The chipped, welted wood stood in stark constant to the white stone, and served as a reminder that even our political discourse exists only because of Rome's past military exploits.

Scipio started up the stairs at the back of the rostra before turning back to us. "I doubt any of these plebs would be brave enough to storm the rostra, but do your best to deter them if any do try."

With that, he turned back up the steps and continued to the platform, joining his brother-in-law Tiberius. As far as I knew, he had prepared nothing in advance, but he seemed confident enough. The weight of his name and the authority of his cause would surely be able to win over even the most loyal of Tiberius' followers. That being said, there was a look in his eye as he reached the height of the platform. Something like an animal when it senses a predator. Or a trap.

"I shall let our illustrious hero begin," Tiberius said, directly to Scipio, but loud enough for most to hear.

Scipio took a few steps to the center of the stage and straightened his back. He clasped the folds of his toga in his left hand, and raised his right arm.

"Citizens of Rome," Scipio began, his voice deep and rough, recalling to mind the orders he once gave on the battlefield. "If I had not been detained in Spain, I would have never allowed things to get this far," he said. He paused and allowed the silence to settle for a moment, conveying the seriousness of the situation.

Unfortunately, a few heckles began, followed by many more. Most were boos and hisses, others shouted "allow?", "he wouldn't allow!", or "he thinks himself a king"! So perhaps saying they remained in "reverential silence" was an exaggeration, but at least they didn't heckle the speakers while they spoke. Few of our citizens show that kind of decency today.

Tiberius remained unaffected, watching his brother-in-law with curiosity and respect.

"I wouldn't have *allowed* it because I would have spoken reason to you sooner. I would not remain with many of my colleagues on the benches of the Senate house, complaining about how this man," and here he pointed to his Tiberius, "is breaking all the rules. No, I would be here, speaking to you about the foolishness of his measures. I have always been honest with you, citizens, and I have always been faithful."

A handful of claps and cheers rose up, including myself and the rest of Scipio's retinue, but it failed to catch on and silence soon followed.

"Foolish. That's what I'd call it. I will not make insinuations about this man's intentions... although I do call into question his methods. I am sure, citizens, that he truly believes in the righteousness of his cause. But he has not considered the implications."

"The nobles! The rich!" the crowds shouted.

Scipio shook his head.

"No, those standing opposed against these measures are not only the wealthy who lead this Republic, those you so detest, but those who have sense enough to realize the ramifications. Who will take away land from the man whose family has tilled that earth since we defeated Hannibal? Their ancestors were awarded this land for their bravery in battle, mind you! Who will take away their land?"

The crowds had little response.

"Their ancestors were brave, not the men themselves!" One voice rose above the rest, but even the mob seemed to groan at this.

"It is sacred tradition to pass down land to one's sons. Why else would a man strive for greatness in this life if it all evaporates with his life?"

Even some of the men who had been jeering at Scipio lifted a gentle applause.

I tapped my foot and bit my nail. I hoped he had the words not only to sway the crowd, but myself as well.

"But even this fact is not what concerns me most. How many of you are farmers?" he asked. A few men raised their arms or grunted. "Show yourselves." A few more joined in. "Farming is hard work. A skill that must be taught from youth, and refined by year after year of sweat and strenuous labor. Who will teach those placed on the state land how to farm it? Who will educate them on how to rear an adequate harvest? Him?" He now pointed at Tiberius once again. "The man has never lifted a plow in his life. And even if he had, he does not possess enough time in his life to teach

each man, even if he spent every breath until his last, attempting to do so."

As I said, there weren't many farmers in the crowd, but he had appealed to the ego of the farmers present, and it wasn't a bad thing to have some in the crowd who agreed with what he said. And all the farmers nodded proudly.

Scipio adjusted his posture and raise his arm to the sky once more, to assert that he was making his closing remarks. "On top of the impossible task of redistributing land that has belonged to certain families for hundreds of years, and teaching the men landowners how to farm it, we must consider how this would impact our Italian allies. Our noble friends are already clamoring, as it will be them who suffer from this the most. That land which we allowed to remain in their possession when we conquered them will be spread out amongst Roman citizens."

Here the heckles began again, and louder now.

"Traitor!"

"Go and be with your *Italians* then!" some of them cried.

Scipio wasn't perturbed. "Citizens, you know that I have been a true Roman from my first breath to my last. But these men are amongst those who purchased, with their blood, the victory over the Numantines and the Carthaginians. I would know. I was the one who led them." The mob will always consider themselves patriots, and so were forced to clap here. "I stand for the rights of my people before all else, but we cannot go about alienating our most loyal allies. So, I move that this legislation be tabled until we have the ability to address all the issues here described... and we have a more able leader to assist in its execution."

Scipio looked at Tiberius, attempting to see if he was

cracking, but he was not. He took a step away from the center and allowed Tiberius to take his place.

Tiberius didn't speak at first. He didn't take the traditional stance of a Roman orator or raise his right arm. Instead he stood, nodding to himself as if in deep thought.

He remained silent until even the quietest of murmurs in the crowd ceased.

"My brother in law speaks sense. He speaks honestly. Before I begin my response, I'd like to thank him for his service to Rome, both with his sword and his voice." He turned to Scipio and clapped, and the crowd followed his example. They cheered Scipio far more at Tiberius' behest then they ever had at the result of his own words.

"Everything he says comes from a noble heart and a wise mind. But," and now he turned again to the crowd and straightened his shoulders, "he has been gone so long that he doesn't know how bad things have become. But I've been here. I've seen what Rome has become. I've seen my brethren dying, bleeding, *starving* and something must be done! There is no time for pointless words. Every moment we delay an effective response to the daily catastrophes we are faced with, the more Romans die!" The crowds roared, not only applause, but cries of anger against the injustice of their positions. "When will we be prepared to "address all the issues here described", and when will a leader be educated enough to address them?"

"Never!"

"It's you Tiberius!" the crowds shouted.

"We cannot wait! There is no time for delay. Rome is faced with Cerberus, a three headed beast: homelessness in this glorious city, a poisonous reliance on other nations for our grain, and not enough land owning citizens for service in the legions. With this one reform I propose, we can address every issue. We give homes to the homeless, rely on their grain rather than Sicily's, and increase the numbers of our land owning veterans. Tell me, brothers, are the problems we are currently faced with not far greater than the issues our hero Scipio has just laid out?" Tiberius asked, and the people all roared their approval.

He had shifted the issue, it wasn't Tiberius versus Scipio anymore. They didn't have to stand against their hero, he was simply misinformed—*away for too long.*

And his next move was a well-timed one. Despite the fact the Scipio had been away with those very legionaries, it was always a positive stratagem to target old legionaries themselves. Not only would this tickle the veterans themselves, but it would sit well with the ordinary citizens themselves, all of which were self-purported patriots.

"And is it not time that our veterans be honored? Honored with land, with roofs over their heads?" I had believed previously that the crowd couldn't get any louder, but I was here proven wrong. "But maybe our learned friend here can tell us otherwise?" Tiberius bowed and gestured to Scipio, as he had seen him shaking his head.

"No one honors the veterans more than I! I am one of them, I have perspired and bled right alongside them! But have we not just witnessed, yesterday, a glorious triumph to honor those same veterans? Rome has always, and *will* always, stand for her legionaries! The rose petals still rest on our very streets!" Scipio said to moderate applause.

The moment it stalled, Tiberius took his place and continued.

"But who paid for that Triumph? Was it not you?" Tiberius exclaimed, as the crowd let out a gasp, which was followed by rancorous laughter. "Everyone knows you paid for the Triumph yourself! You might honor Rome's veterans, Scipio, but Rome's elite have long ceased to do so! And it is time that changed!" The crowd reached the height of their ovations.

Tiberius' eyes shone. Why else would he have allowed Scipio a chance to speak when he had the floor, unless he had anticipated this? They had the same argument the night previous, and Tiberius had kept his response for this moment. In one powerful sentence he had allowed the crowd to still adore their hero but continue to clamor for Tiberius' measures. Such a powerful orator, I'm convinced there never was. He was always a few steps ahead.

"Rose petals will not feed their children! It will not shelter them from the cold nor heat!" Tiberius shouted over the roars. "Therefore, I propose that my measure be carried to fruition and the people, you, be allowed to vote on its legitimacy. You, Romans, can decide which issues the Republic should be forced to handle moving forward. The ones laid out by myself, or those presented by my friend and colleague Scipio Aemilianus. It is up to you!" He bowed, the rapturous applause not stunted in the least.

Both men exited the platform. Tiberius was swallowed up by his own men and their congratulations, and Scipio by his.

"Powerful words, general," I said, along with the others in his entourage. We clapped him on the back and pandered to his ego as if he had won the debate, but he had not, and his face revealed that he knew it.

Everything Scipio said was logical. But Tiberius said what the people wanted to hear. Even I, to my shame, had felt myself agreeing with the revolutionary tribune. But of course, I never said that. I slapped Scipio's shoulder and told him how well he had done, just as everyone else.

I wondered how many of his other followers were swayed as well, despite how fervently they supported him.

Scipio was sweating, and his hands tremored.

"Marius, I want you to accompany me to the Senate House tomorrow. And bring your sword," he said, his breath labored. "I've never feared the war cry of my enemies, and I won't now be frightened by the wails of these step-children of Italy... but it's been a long time since I've truly known my brother-by-law..." Scipio looked down, and there was sadness in his eyes. "And I don't know what he's capable of."

"Yes, general," was my only response. But I hoped there would be no confrontation on the way to the Senate house, because I no longer knew what side of the conflict I truly stood on.

War is always simpler than politics. As I'm sure you'll soon find out.

Scipio ensured that we were among the first to arrive at the senate house the next morning. They were meeting that day in the Temple of Castor and Pollux, and Scipio declined to convene with his senatorial allies at the nearby *senaculum* beforehand as was his custom. He was anxious and I could sense it. His eyes shifted all about him as we walked, as they had when we scoured the tree line for Numantia's warriors. He rubbed his neck often, as if the muscles had tightened up into knots.

Every time we had marched or ridden into battle together, Scipio had been the same: calm, collected, and alert. Now he was different. He seemed more nervous marching to the senate house than he had into the fray of battle. What was he frightened of? It couldn't possible be a fear of death by one of Tiberius' loyalists in the crowd. A dagger in Rome feels no different than a dagger in Spain. What was it then? Does he fear the loss of his reputation? Disrespect to his name? Was he fearful that the nobles would lose their republic to the likes of Tiberius? Or was he simply not confident in the validity of his cause?

He tried to be courteous to those we passed along the way, but the moment they asked about his debate with Tiberius or his intentions moving forward, he stepped past them and continued on his way with only a curt nod as a response.

When we reached the stone steps of the temple, Scipio continued and I remained behind, as only members of the senatorial order were allowed to pass that sacred boundary. Others gathered behind and beside me, anxious to hear the proceedings of the day. I had never attended a meeting of the senate before, but I had to imagine there were more attending this day than was typical. There was a nervous buzz of energy surrounding the building, and it grew each time a member of the senate passed through our midst through those doors and found his seat.

Tiberius was amongst the last to arrive, but certainly created the most excitement. Rather than applause, there were gasps, as if he were a mythological creature come to life. As if they believed him to be a thing of legend. But here he now stood in the flesh, as real as a man can be.

He alone seemed unaffected by the stress of the day, taking the time to shake the hands of those closest to him, and addressing many by name and asking about the state of their affairs or the health of their wives and children.

At last he passed through our midst and into the temple, surrounded by those who hated him most, as carelessly as a carpenter sitting down at his workbench.

Several of the men and woman gathered there tried to squirm past me, but I used some of the intimidation tactics I had learned in Spain to keep my place. I was determined to have a front row to the fate of the Republic, if it was to be decided this day.

The proceedings of the day began slowly. That month's presiding consul took the floor and laid out the topics of discussion, careful to glance at his co-consul seated directly before him, where they communicated with gestures and a nod of the head. There were several items on the day's agenda, but most of them pertaining to foreign emissaries or other administrative necessities. Even the crusty old men who typically reveled in such monotony tapped their feet anxiously, stealing glances to the floor where Tiberius sat on a bench with the nine other tribunes.

After all the other issues were out of the way, the topic of Tiberius' land redistribution legislation was finally on the table.

The presiding consul, Calpurnius Piso, spoke first.

"I consider this piece of legislation an affront to the Roman constitution, and the *mos maiorum* everything we have was built upon." This generated a few nervous chuckles, since it was his friend Gaius Laelius who first proposed the measure to the Senate before they shut him down. "It is not the land redistribution that I find unfit, it is the man who proposes it. I, above all else, should have the respect of this august body for opposing it, since it is a measure which I sought to pass myself." He now turned to Tiberius. "But I respect this house. And I listened to my elders both in years and in experience. If only the same could be said for this boy," he said, flicking his wrist at Tiberius in distaste. "But instead he has pissed on this house, pissed on our tradition—"

"This topic is not about my means, which were constitutional in and of themselves, but about the legislation," Tiberius rose to his feet and cut off the consul coldly.

"And if only we needed more proof, he has given it to us! The consul has the floor, boy, not you!" The other leading member of the Scipiones, Scipio Nasica, shouted.

"That's tribune to you, if you please," Tiberius corrected, returning to his seat.

"Consul Piso still has the floor,"

"I have nothing further to say. This bill cannot be passed, if only to prevent the precedence of circumventing the senate and going directly before the mob... and the precedence of spoiled young men spitting on their leadership. Before long, we may be paying homage to those still in on their mother's teat." Piso took his seat to applause and sparse laughter, but the mood was too tense for it to catch on.

The other Proconsuls were given the opportunity to speak, and each said the same thing. They were repulsed by Tiberius' tactics, and some said more poignantly that they were repulsed by the man himself.

The Pontifex Maximus Scipio Nasica was the most long-winded of the bunch, giving his fellow senators a lengthy exhortation about the tradition of the ancestors and how morals lay at the root of Rome's success. Few listened. It was almost time for the tribune himself to speak, and everyone was anxious to hear what he had to say.

I thought, presumably with everyone else, that Scipio would not be addressing the matter. Everyone around him was tugging on his toga, imploring, begging him to stand up. But he exhaled and shook his head.

In irritation, and only after ignoring them for some time, did the general stand to his feet.

"Honor demands honesty. I will address something before I speak. Tiberius bested me in debate yesterday." I expected a few laughs, but there were none. "He is a brilliant orator, that, none of us can take from him. He knows what the people want to hear, he understands their desire." He paused for a moment here, and turned his entire body towards his brother-in-law across the senate floor. "Tiberius, this may work for twenty years. Perhaps even thirty. But eventually this will all crumble down around us. And it will be the very people you seek to appease that will suffer the brunt of the consequences. An even more ambitious man will take your place. And that man's measures will not fall within the confines of land redistribution. In time this senate will be no more, and there will only be the most crafty and witty man at the pinnacle of power. He will rule the seven hills and all the glory here contained."

With that, Scipio took his seat. All eyes shifted to the Tribune, who nodded his head with interest and respectful consideration.

It was the first time his measure had been brought up before the Senate while he was there to defend it. And at last he would address the words spoken against him.

He stood to his feet and adjusted himself as he had on the rostra the previous evening. He again waited for total silence.

"Conscript Fathers, I am honored to speak with you today." A few murmurs of incredulity began, but the force of Tiberius' voice was too commanding to be drowned out. "And I am honored to be able to correct you. You remain here, in this holy place, speaking of my legislation as if it were still yours to decide upon. But the people have already spoken. You have no more say in the matter." He paused and let the full measure of his words sink in, the fat old senators gasping and choking on his insolence. "I will tell all of you the same thing I told our conquering hero, my brother-in-law Scipio Aemilianus: if you can convince the people that they are wrong, and their opinions change, I will repeal my own law before it is voted upon tomorrow. Otherwise, you are too late."

"May I remind you," one of the other tribunes stood to his feet. Although it was quite a distance away from my position outside the senate house, I recalled the man as Marcus Octavius, one of Scipio's dinner guests the night prior. "You are not the only man who speaks for the people, colleague."

Tiberius pondered the man with intense curiosity.

"And when the measure is put to a vote tomorrow, I will use my tribune's veto to block it."

Two-thirds of the chamber immediately erupted in applause. The other third, Tiberius' loyal supporters, the Claudians, stood to their feet and shouted over themselves at the hapless tribune. Neither of these bodies of senators could drown out the roar of the mob surrounding me. Octavius stood there with his eyes downcast, but saying nothing more.

For the first time, Tiberius truly appeared stunned. He had been bested, it seemed. His vascular forearms flexed and the muscles in his neck twitched. For a moment he was at a total loss for words, but fortunately the roar of both senatorial parties continued for some time.

"You will veto the motion?" Tiberius asked as the roar continued.

"I will!" Octavius exclaimed as the tumult picked up again.

Tiberius picked up his feet and strode for the exit.

Both parties instantly fell silent.

"You have the floor, Tribune, speak!" the consul shouted. But he did not pause.

As he exited, myself and the other gatherers parted as if he were a high priest or a leper, unwilling to touch him or impede his path.

Had he really given up so easily?

We watched as he paced away from the Temple of Castor and Pollux, even the senators pouring out from their seats to join us.

But he didn't take the path to the right, leading to his mother's home on the Palatine. Instead, he walked straight up the steps to the Rostra.

He stood as still as his broken statues now do, and waited for a crowd to assemble.

He said nothing for a long while.

"Marcus Octavius!" He shouted. We waited for something to follow. "Marcus Octavius!" He bellowed again, like a general crying for the head of an enemy king. "Marcus Octavius!"

Now the people began to rally his cry, like the general's finest men.

"Marcus Octavius! Marcus Octavius!" They shouted out.

I turned back to the temple just in time to see Octavius being pushed from the midst of the senators. They may have been supporting him, but he would have to stand alone.

He walked slowly, reluctantly, towards the rostra. His eyes darted this way and that, searching for a means of escape, but on every side the people cried out his name.

"Marcus Octavius says he will veto my law as you, the people, vote upon it tomorrow!" Tiberius said as his colleague joined him on the platform. "And is it your will that my legislation be vetoed?" The people roared in disapproval. Tiberius paced over to Octavius and talked with him quietly for a moment. I could see, even from that distance, that Octavius was shaking.

When they had finished speaking, Tiberius squeezed his eyes shut and shook his head in bitter disappointment.

"And who votes to elect the tribunes?" Tiberius asked the mob.

"Us!" The people roared.

"And who are they supposed to speak for?"

"Us!"

"If it is just, then, that the people should elect those who should defend their rights, how much more just is it that the people should have the right to depose the man who actively fights against them!" The whole city gasped. Head's turned as everyone wondered what he was proposing. We believed we understood, but such a measure had never been presented in Rome's history. "One of us has sold out. Sold out like a prostitute in an Aventine brothel. Either myself or Octavius has abused his power as tribune and has forgotten who elected him, and who he is to protect!"

"It's him, it's him!"

"It's not you, Tiberius!" the people cried.

"Therefore," Tiberius adjusted himself and raised his arm as if this little bout of oratory had been planned, "I propose that tomorrow we vote instead on which tribune should be able to continue in his role. One of us does not stand for the will of the people. The other does. Only one will remain. And a week hence, my bill will be voted on. And it will be carried or squashed by the *will of the people*!"

Octavius remained where he was, planted like a root, flabbergasted. His mouth open like a sea-bass. If he and the nobles had surprised Tiberius, then their efforts had been paid back in full.

The senate rushed down from the temple, forgetting that their session had not been officially concluded, to heckle down their enemy. But he had already departed. Surrounded by his loyal patriots, he was already well on his way home before the horde of senators had made it to the rostra.

Scipio Aemilianus remained in the Senate house, seated on his bench with his hands in his lap.

I believe he alone saw what was coming next. And he did not like it.

I FOLLOWED Aemilianus and his retinue back to his palace on the Palatine, passing by roving hordes of the people who were celebrating as if the *praecones* had just announced the conquest of a foreign enemy. And who could blame them? The nobles had made their last attempt to block their hero's measures, and he had outwitted them all. And the way he spoke, he made it clear that it was their victory rather than his, almost as if he hadn't even devised the plan to begin with. He was just a spokesman. Although any man with half a brain could see that wasn't the case, he was talented at maintaining that appearance before those who did not.

Not long after we returned home, several litters appeared at our doorsteps. As far as I knew, Scipio hadn't sent for any of them, but the senatorial leaders knew exactly where to go to strategize their defense. It wasn't long before Scipio's tablinum was bustling with Rome's finest and their secretaries. Among them were Gaius Laelius and the

Pontifex Maximus, Scipio Nasica, both pale as ghosts and trembling with anger.

"Where's Octavius?" Laelius asked, his voice calmer than his eye portrayed.

Out of the noble men gathered, he was the only one without a lineage tracing back to Rome's founding. In fact, he was descended from shepherds. His father had been a devoted friend and ally of Scipio Africanus, however, and that made him fit for such fine company. Regardless, it appeared to me that he had more nobility in his little finger than the others possessed throughout their rotund bodies. His face was etched like his late father's statue with strength and dignity. He had a strong, bovine jaw line but his small brown eyes shone with wisdom and consideration.

"I instructed him not to come, for his safety," Scipio Aemilianus replied, slouching in his chair and rubbing his temples.

"For ours, you mean," Scipio Nasica said, crossing his arms. The Pontifex Maximus and former consul was an odd looking man, to say the least. He had a compressed face that seemed too small for his head. His lips were perpetually pursed like he had just bitten into a sour grape, and his nose was long and beaked, always turned up at others. His frame wasn't adequately designed to uphold the body fat he had collected in his old age, his bone-thin hands serving as a reminder of a slender youth long behind him.

"If the mob catches wind that we had anything to do with his position, they might not stop with voting him out of office. They might bludgeon him to death in the streets... such an event wouldn't seem out of place these days."

"He's probably right, our best chance of success is if the people can believe the man acted on his own volition and truly believes the bill is against them. Perhaps they can at least sympathize with the man." Laelius placed a hand on his chin.

"Did that seem like a sympathetic crowd to you?" Nasica bellowed, stepping closer to the proconsul and forcing him to meet his eyes. It seemed he was unused to being politically outwitted, and he didn't know how to contain his repulsion.

Scipio Aemilianus simply seemed exhausted. Beaten, he sunk further in his chair and rolled his eyes as other voices of concern and consternation rose around the room.

I stopped paying attention. My mind drifted to simpler things, and I considered what I had missed over the past few weeks. Perhaps my daughter had learned to say a few new words. Perhaps she was beginning to see her uncle as her father. Perhaps her wobble had become a walk.

"We have a spy in our midst," Nasica's stern voice jarred me from my thoughts. For a moment, I thought they were talking about me. My face turned as pink as the autumn peach.

"I'm no spy, dear cousin," a soft voice came from the back of the room. All eyes turned to Sempronia, who had seated herself in the back of the room behind the bloated bodies of Rome's elite.

"You'll call me Pontifex Maximus, damn you. And I'm not your cousin, I'm your husband's. And if he were to ask me, the marriage between you two was crafted by evil spirts." Nasica turned to his cousin. "I don't want her here, Aemilianus. She'll report everything we say to her damn brother."

"I'm a dutiful wife," Sempronia said, not without humor in her eyes. "And if there are conspiracies of the state involving my husband, I believe I should be well informed."

"Get out, Sempronia," Scipio flicked his hand to the

door. His irritation with his comrades was compounded by his wife's inquisition.

"See how brave this man is." She stood and gestured to her husband. Her beauty was striking in a room full of balding and puffy men in togas. "He can fight off enemies in every corner of the Republic but he can't stand up to the nobles who berate his wife." She turned and began to walk out, "He's a coward."

One any other occasion, Scipio would have been expected to respond to such flagrant disrespect from a member of his household, but he resigned to handle one catastrophe at a time.

"He simply cannot do this, Aemilianus. There is no precedent for ousting a tribune in all the Republic's history. I've consulted the annals. There is nothing that justifies this treason." Nasica slammed his fists on the desk, in an attempt to wake up the general, as if he weren't already aware.

"And is there any law that specifically states he cannot? If we had longer to strategize I'm certain we'd develop a plan to stop this, but we do not. The bastard is clever, I'll give him that. I'm beginning to suspect he saw this coming all along. He knew tomorrow was an auspicious day for voting, but he never intended to have his legislation passed tomorrow... he was waiting until we showed our hand." Scipio Aemilianus met the gaze of the Pontifex Maximus. He didn't reproach his cousin's obnoxious behavior, but those piercing eyes forced him to recoil.

"So who has a suggestion? Who has a plan? Or did you all gather here to remind me of the situation I was present to witness just hours ago?" Aemilianus said, finally standing to his feet.

He looked around the room, gesturing to each man in turn, but none gave any suggestions.

"You paying attention, lad? You'll have to deal with this one day too," Aemilianus turned to me. I shuffled nervously and swelled with pride, as that comment confirmed what he once said about me around a campfire in Spain: that perhaps I would one day be his successor.

"I have an idea," I said. I instantly regretted it, but I wanted to capitalize on my general's trust.

"That's more than the rest of these noblemen, so speak," Aemilianus said.

"Both men could sacrifice their *sacrosanctitas*. One of them will lose it tomorrow, but Octavius can speak up before the vote and offer that they both lose it. Then they can duel. The victor will be revealed to be the gods' favored."

There was silence for a moment, before the room erupted with laughter. Only Scipio Aemilianus wasn't slapping his knee in condescension.

"Who on Gaia's earth is this brute? And why is he here?" Nasica asked.

"Often times I wish we were still in Spain, where that is exactly how disputes such as this would be handled. Unfortunately, we are not," Scipio said, glaring at those who were mocking me.

"Truly, thank you, young man. We did need something to cheer us up a bit." Nasica wiped a tear from his eye.

"A duel is something the *hoi polloi* can understand. It would expose Tiberius for a coward if he refused," I responded, my eyes locked on Nasica, although I recoiled a bit, stinging with embarrassment.

"Perhaps the goat fuckers from whatever hole you came from would accept such a barbaric idea, but the Roman populace, despite all their depravation, are at least civilized," Nasica said, as coolly as if he were speaking of the weather.

Scipio Aemilianus held his hand out to stop me before I replied.

"Gaius Marius is a guest in my home and I won't have him slandered here. Do you understand?" Scipio's voice contained as much conviction as it did on the battlefield.

"He'll defend his ill born soldiers but not his wife," Nasica whispered to Laelius, but loud enough for all to hear.

"Get out!" Scipio slammed his fist onto the desk. "Get out now. All of you!"

The remained still as statues for an extended moment, utterly shocked at the outburst. Scipio was typically a well-composed man, and his anger was quite threatening.

"It was just jesting between cousins." Nasica shrugged.

"Out! Out! Come back to me when any of you have something more constructive than insults and incessant wailing."

They slowly poured into the atrium and out to the exit. Nasica was the last to leave.

"You're not a general any longer, little cousin. I'm the High Priest of Rome. And I needn't remind you that Rome's menace right now is your brother-in-law, and a man who's career you helped build. You should be the one with the ideas." Nasica spun on his heels and exited before Aemilianus replied.

The erstwhile general remained silent, breathing heavily, as he balanced himself with both hands on his desk, his chin tucked to his chest.

"I have another idea, general,"

"Oh, gods, I love it when you call me that. It's days like these that I miss being in the field, where I'd bugger boys like Tiberius for breakfast, and where the haughtiness of men like my cousin are noticeably absent. Tell me your idea, Tribune."

"You have many soldiers in the city, still celebrating after the triumph. Not only will they vote how you tell them, but they presumably still have their swords as well... and angry, armed men can often sway a vote in other ways."

Scipio spun in his chair and locked eyes with me for a long time. It was a treasonous idea, I'll admit, but he was at least considering it.

It was late March at the time, and I've learned since that Rome was typically already sweltering with heat and humidity by that time of year. But as we poured out of Scipio's home just after dawn the following morning, there was a bitter nip in the air. The sun had risen but was blocked by grey, foreboding clouds. There was a silent hope that perhaps a storm would soon be upon us, and the augurs might declare the day inauspicious.

There was an idea: they could have bought the augurs for a marginal sum, and had the vote postponed a week or so, giving them enough time to formulate a defense for Octavius. But, alas, the chief augur was a Claudian, and they were still loyal to Tiberius at the time. Even if a storm appeared, there was no telling if they would postpone the vote. Ice might have rained down from the skies, or a bird flying with a snake in its talons might be spotted overtop the capital, but it was unlikely anything would be done about it.

It's interesting how religion and politics are intermingled so.

Scipio's retinue was larger that day than I had ever

recalled. They wore cloaks, presumably for the cold, but it wasn't difficult to spot the hilts of swords beneath them.

And the closer we came to the Field of Mars, where the vote would take place, the more and more armed men I spotted. Their hair was cut short and they stood in a way that only soldiers know how.

I grinned when I realized Scipio had taken my advice. He must have sent out envoys in the night. I was grinning, sure, but my heartbeat was speeding up by the second, as I realized what this might mean.

I was surprised to see very few of Rome's senators and magistrates present. It was an assembly of the people, so they couldn't bring with them their symbols of office or their lictors. They were only permitted to attend as ordinary citizens. That being said, for such a monumental occasion, I expected to see more of a presence from the nobility.

It made me think they sensed danger in the air and desired to stay as far away from it as possible, within the warmth of their domi, with their doors barred.

"Ay there, general, how you votin' today?" plebs asked Aemilianus as we marched by. Others laughed.

Stealing a glance, I noticed that these men, too, were armed. Some had the broken legs of desks or benches, others with a candle holder or a dagger. The only thing more intimidating than a body of soldiers is a mass of hungry, armed men.

"General," I said, hurrying up to Aemilianus and placing a hand on his shoulder.

He kept his gaze forward.

"I see them. How many do you count?" he whispered, appearing unperturbed.

I scanned on either side of Aemilianus' retinue.

"Too difficult to count. They're not uniformed. They might all be armed for all I can tell."

"Then we'll have to assume they are."

What kind of conflict would we be faced with if the vote turned sour? How many bodies would litter Rome's streets? The eternal city had never been exposed to her own blood. Romans hadn't raised their hand against Romans within the city confines since Romulus killed his brother Remus at Rome's founding.

Only I was close enough to notice how Scipio's skin was twitching.

When we arrived at the Field of Mars, I spotted the accused tribune standing on a raised platform before the booths constructed for voting. Poor Octavius looked like he had seen Medusa, frozen in stone, his gaze cast out before the populace who clearly saw him as inadequate.

The mob was less talkative then it typically was. Perhaps they sensed danger too. Everyone seemed to be whispering, only to those closest to them, conspiracies being passed along in secret. Everyone was quiet, that is, except for the intimidators, who were stationed along the voting booths, just far enough away to safely get away with their behavior.

"Who are you voting for little man? The Republic doesn't forget traitors. We kill them," I heard some of them say as the populace lined up in their 35 tribes.

"Do we have men doing the same?" I asked Scipio.

"We do. But I see far more of Tiberius' ilk. Don't you?" He replied, his voice even.

"I do."

"Well, it won't matter. The moment I snap my fingers men will spring up all over Mar's field," he said, his voice quieter now. I assume he was speaking symbolically now. I hoped he hadn't taken my advice too literally. Intimidation was one thing, butchery was another. I couldn't believe Scipio would make such an order, but prolonged absence in warfare can create such brutality in a man. And for that reason, I had no doubt that my brothers would obey if that order was in fact given.

But then Tiberius arrived. I couldn't see him for quite some time before the crowd of people, but it was clear he was arriving. The nervous murmur of the crowds dissolved into silence. All I heard was the marching of Tiberius' massive retinue.

Retinue doesn't quite describe it. A small army, more like. Tiberius walked from the center of this formation, a hand lifted in exultation to the crowds who loved him. Some of them reached out to touch him or craned their heads to see him, but it was nearly impossible. If there was an attempt on his life, the assassins would have to cut down a hundred men or more before they got to him.

The men in the front of the formation were clad in cloaks and hoods, but it was easy to see the glimmer of armor beneath them.

They maintained their ranks until the frontline of men had pushed and shoved their way directly to the platform. They parted ranks and allowed the Tribune to exit their ranks untouched. He began to ascend the steps, but then his gaze shifted right towards us. My palms began to sweat as I felt his gaze piercing into me. I looked back and forth, trying to determine who he was looking at, and my breath quickened as he descended the steps again and approached, a few of his armored men stepping closer to us as well.

"How do you like them?" Tiberius asked his brother-in-law as he approached, to my relief.

"They look like lictors. You break so many laws it is becoming difficult to keep count."

"I've broken no laws, brother," Tiberius said with a smile, as composed and calm as a cup of water.

"Brother by law," Scipio replied, his eye's locked with the tribune's. "The people love you today. But they will come to see what you truly are. In time they will see this little horde of thugs as an affront to their freedom. And when that day comes, you'll be left alone, and helpless. And I will not be there to save you."

"Save me? When have you *ever* saved me?" Tiberius asked, incredulous, his voice cracking for the first time. He stepped closer, compelling myself and Scipio's other allies to step closer around him.

"After your surrender to the Numantines years ago. If it wasn't for me—"

"If it wasn't for you?" Tiberius shouted, the veins in his neck bulged and his eyes surged with fury. I had never seen him like that before. Without thinking, I reached for the dagger on my hip and placed a hand on its hilt. "I had brokered peace with the enemy! I saved an entire Roman army from dishonor and death! And you betrayed me! You insulted me before the senate."

"I saved you from the senate! If it wasn't for me, they would have sent you naked and in chains back to the enemy along with your commander Mancinus."

"I have informants everywhere. I know it was you who led the assault on my peace treaty." Tiberius trembled with repressed anger. I fixed my hand around the hilt, fully preparing for Tiberius to lunge for Scipio over his support- ers. "And that was the day I realized I couldn't trust my 'brother by law', that I can't trust anyone. And I decided to take my own path." Tiberius stopped and his red face cooled. He smiled then and gestured to the mob around us.

"Your own path is fraught with corruption and violence. And it will end in your death," Scipio said, composing himself as well. Tiberius' white teeth shone in the morning light as he laughed. Then he turned back to the steps. "These thugs have guaranteed it."

Tiberius spun on his heels and approached Scipio even closer than before. I brandished my dagger but kept it hidden beneath the folds of my cloak. But the tribune approached so calmly, no one stopped him.

He placed a hand around Scipio's neck and looked deep into his eyes.

"No, they have saved me from death. Scipio, when a pigeon dies on the Aventine, I hear of it. So, do not be surprised when you find that I'm informed about the presence of your soldiers here at this sacred vote. I have soldiers of my own, but they fight for a cause rather than a man. If it's blood you want, you shall have it. But I'd encourage you to stand down." Tiberius leaned in and kissed Scipio firmly on both cheeks, before turning and striding up the steps to the platform. He paused at the top and inhaled deeply. His composure returned like a current on the Italian shoreline.

"Let the vote begin!" He raised his arms to the air like a priest, and the people roared in response.

One by one, the tribes were called to the voting booth. The nippy air of the morning dissipated into humid heat, not the least because of the sweating bodies of all those surrounding us. It took quite some time for all 35 tribes to vote, but there was certainly no deliberation from the voters. They knew exactly who they were voting for.

"Perhaps we should leave. These men look at you like a lion does a deer," some of Scipio's retinue pleaded with them, gesturing to Tiberius' horde who eyed us from nearby.

"No. If we're to be defeated, I will look my enemy in his eye. And I will remember this moment when I stand over him, victorious."

The urban praetor read the votes aloud, starting with the first tribe. When 17 of the 35 votes were announced, all had voted for Octavius to be removed. One more, and the vote would be complete.

"Stop! Stop! Stop!" Tiberius shouted, waving his arms and approaching the praetor. The nervous magistrate looked around for some counsel, but once the mob rallied the Tribune's cry, he nodded his consent.

Tiberius took center stage, and turned to his fellow tribune Marcus Octavius.

"It is clear how the people feel. Please, stop this madness! Relent and step down from your position as tribune of plebs."

"No," was all the hapless Octavius mustered.

"Take a moment and look out into this crowd," Tiberius said, wrapping an arm around Octavius' shoulder and pointing out to the masses before them.

"How many of the noblemen who bought you are here now? Let me tell you this, as I know these men well, the moment this vote continues and you are removed from your office, they will abandon you! You will be no more use to them. They will cast you aside as a mother does her child's shit and piss. And you will be left all alone!"

"No," Octavius replied again. Some of the people began to jeer at him, but Tiberius waved for them to cease.

"But the people, these people, they are loyal! If you step down and allow their bill to pass, they will welcome you with open arms as a repentant man, as a hero of their cause!" Tiberius swung an arm out towards the people, "Won't you?"

"Yes!"

"We will!"

They shouted their reply. Tiberius waited for it to dissipate.

"Your dedication is admirable. But you stand for the wrong cause, and you know that now. Step down, Octavius, and rejoin the ranks of those who voted for you!"

"He wishes to avoid the ramifications of his actions. The moment his term of office expires, we'll have him thrown off the Tarpeian Rock for this," Scipio said. The general swallowed hard, nervous that the poor tribune might take Tiberius' advice.

"No," Octavius said, looking to his red slippers, unable to meet the gaze of the now bloodthirsty onlookers.

"Then I wash my hands of this! Let the voting continue!" Tiberius threw up his arms, revealing a bit of his anger once more.

Predictably, the next tribe's vote was for Octavius to be removed from his office.

Scipio turned and pushed through us the moment the vote was announced. We followed closely behind him, myself especially, as I scanned the faces of those closest by us, my hand still gripping the hilt of my dagger.

"*Perduellio*, the most ancient form of treason. That's what we'll have him tried for the moment his term of office is over," Scipio said, mostly to himself. If he was afraid of the mob around us, he did not show it, shoving through anyone who stood in his way.

Behind us, Octavius was dragged, kicking and screaming, from the platform. None of us turned around to watch.

But I can still remember the sound of his wails ringing out across the Field of Mars.

Later that day, once we were far from that Field of Mars and its hordes of Tiberius loyalists, a vote took place for the Tribune to take Octavius place.

The man who took office was Tiberius' little brother, Gaius Gracchus. Needless to say, no one else would be vetoing Tiberius' legislation again.

PART II

*W*ithout another tribune to block his bill, Tiberius' legislation became law. It was a complete and utter victory for the young tribune, but by the time the voting began, all the nobles had prepared themselves for the outcome. There were no shaking fists, curses, or angry rants from the rostra. Instead, the nobles met the unanimous vote for their enemy's proposal with solemn faces and downcast eyes.

To crown his achievement, within the week a further measure was passed in Tiberius' favor. A commission was assembled to oversee the land redistribution, as was customary. But who would lead it? Before Tiberius was finished, he, his little brother Gaius, and Tiberius' father-in-law Appius Claudius were all elected to the commission.

He quickly left the city to begin his work before the glory of his achievement was tarnished in any way.

The nobles had been beaten. And publicly they gave the appearance that they understood this, but privately (and I know because I was there) Scipio and the other nobles conspired together and encouraged one another to bide their time.

The weeks turned to months, and still I remained in Aemilianus' domus. Several times I mentioned that I should be leaving. I mentioned receiving letters from my cousin who inquired about my delay, but each time Scipio replied the same way, "Not yet, young warrior. We still have work to do."

In truth, my cousin only wrote to tell me how much she enjoyed little Maria. She was barren, and they had no children of their own, so having a babe warmed their hearth fire. Unfortunately for myself, it was the exact warmth that Rome now seemed to lack.

From time to time, I'd sneak off to the quarters Scipio had assigned me, and sit at the foot of my bed. I'd balance my gladius within my hands. It was the only thing that felt like home now. My brother-in-law Gratidius purchased it for me in Genoa, on our way to Spain, when I didn't have enough money to afford a sharp one myself. I could have purchased another one, a far nicer one, now. To be certain I could find one with fewer nicks in the steel. But that sword had shed the blood of my enemy: it was the only thing on Gaia's earth I shared that in common with.

But when I was finished testing its weight and trying to remember what it was like to stand against an enemy in glorious combat, I would place it back in its sheath, and slide the sheath under the bed. It was difficult fighting an enemy with words rather than with the sword. Especially when the enemy wasn't a man at all, but boredom, ambiguity, and apprehension.

To my shame, I believe I began to resent Scipio Aemilianus a bit at the time. It wasn't because of his political stringency, but because he wouldn't let me leave. And because I couldn't figure out why in Jupiter's name he was keeping me there to begin with.

I imagined that living within the home of Scipio would have given me all the satisfaction I desired in the world. If anyone would have told me I would have spent that summer dining with the nobles, being included in their political strategizing, I would have told you this would have been the crowning moment of my life. But I found something to be lacking.

Perhaps I had anticipated that Scipio and I would have spent our evenings recollecting the bravest feats of our recent campaign, or fantasize about future wars where the both of us might earn further glory together. But, in fact, most of our time was spent with waiting. Waiting for what, I was unsure, but I perceived that Scipio had something in mind.

And none of this is to say that Scipio was idle. Waiting, perhaps, but not slothful. At least once a week Nasica, Laelius, and a handful of other nobles would visit for dinner, where they would discuss current events and how they might better position themselves.

Up until this point, their best idea came from Nasica, who proposed that they pass a special legislation to limit the compensation for Tiberius, Gaius, and Appius Claudius to six sestercii per day. This was an insulting low sum, of course, but that's all it was: an insult. It didn't change current affairs whatsoever.

But by early July, their demeanor began to change. The solemnness in their eyes had transformed into anticipation. Perhaps whatever they had been waiting for was finally at hand.

"Have you heard the people clamoring?" Nasica said,

smacking his lips as he chewed on a handful of grapes. "Before long they'll be calling for his head."

I felt myself balking, but was careful to hide it. It had been some time since I had attended a vote or an assembly of the people, but it was difficult to contemplate the people turning on their savior.

"The people will always complain about something. They won't soon betray him," Laelius replied, and I found myself nodding along.

"You're small minded, Laelius. Nothing dries quicker than tears, be they from sadness or joy. In time they'll forget all his fine words and passionate speeches. You just don't contain the foresight to see it. They'll be howling for his blood within the month," Nasica said, just playfully enough to avoid offending his friend.

"Is that what your auguries tell you?" Scipio Aemilianus said without a drop of humor in his voice. Nasica grunted and continued to gorge on his grapes. "I don't agree that the people will turn on Tiberius as quickly as my dear cousin believes, but perhaps now is the opportunity to strike back."

"And what do you suggest?" Marcus Octavius, the deposed tribune, asked. After a lengthy hiatus, which allowed tempers to cool, he had reappeared at Scipio's door, more anxious than ever to see Tiberius' shamed.

"The plebs at large likely haven't altered their support for Tiberius one bit. But those within the city, those who attend the assemblies, are the ones who have yet to receive land. Even if Tiberius' redistribution had taken half of the city population and given them great villas and herds of cattle, those who remained in the city would still feel slighted."

"He didn't promise them all land," Laelius said cautiously.

"No, but he didn't have to. Those peasants weren't clamoring for other peasants to receive farms, but to receive farms of their own. They don't care about the welfare of the state. They wouldn't give a brass obol for the nation's hunger as long as their own bellies are filled.

"Tiberius didn't have to tell each man individually that they'd receive a farm, they all believed or hoped for it in their hearts. And those that Tiberius hasn't selected in his generosity and kindness of spirit, are angry. They feel betrayed. They're furious that the fellow they used to steal bread crumbs with now has food on the table and a shelter over his head. And they'll blame Tiberius." I felt a tinge of anger swelling in my belly. Was that all Tiberius' cause was? A measure to placate the greedy? I felt a little naive and ashamed of myself as well. If only Tiberius was there to answer for himself and the people, or to give one of his rousing speeches. I was certain even then that the man's words could sway me.

"Now you're beginning to see." Nasica grinned and pointed a boney finger at his cousin.

"But what do we *do* about it?"

"I'll make a speech. From the rostra—"

"You're quite brave to return there after your last showing," Nasica interrupted and winked at Laelius. They might have been cousins and political allies, but I could see on Aemilianus's face that Nasica's familiarity was wearing him thin.

"I'll make a speech from the rostra. And there is only one question I need to ask: *how many of you have received farms?* That is all I'll have to ask." Scipio wiped his fingers off on a towel and sat back in his seat, satisfied.

"How many of you have received farms?" Nasica

repeated, his wrinkled eyelids squinting as he attempted to understand.

"That's it. Not a man in the entire crowd will raise their hands."

"How can you insure that?" Octavius asked.

"Boy, you really are dimwitted! If they had received farms from the commission they'd be on them, not in Rome! It doesn't matter how many farms the newsreaders announce have been allocated by Tiberius. The plebs here weren't among them," Nasica said, as pleased with his answer as if he had come up with idea himself.

"That's correct. It will light the spark of fear that Tiberius has abandoned them and forsaken their cause. I'll add a little wood to the fire by mentioning how he is gallivanting across Italy like a king, with all authority to determine who has shelter and who does not. A simple hint that it is actually his spoiled little brother Gaius and that miserly old fool Appius Claudius who have benefited most from this reform, and they'll turn on him. I'm sure of it."

"How many of you have received farms?" Nasica said with a grin, quite pleased with how it sounded. "It's brilliant. Simple, but brilliant. It takes a simple concept for the people to truly respond. Anything more complex and they're left scratching their lice-infested heads. How long did it take you to come up with this little stratagem?"

"Weeks. Months. Too long." Aemilianus stood and turned away from them. "We've grown complacent, men. We've become Rome's greatest complainers but have forgotten how to control our own Republic. If Rome falls to the likes of Tiberius, it isn't the boy's fault, but our own."

"It doesn't matter who came up with the idea, or how long it took. It sounds to me like it will work. And unless the Pontifex Maximus has any objections, I think we know our path forward. We'll begin spreading the message to our own people, and before long the message will be painted on every wall in the city," Laelius said. Nasica grunted again.

"See that it's done. I'll be retiring for the night. You can see yourselves out." Scipio drained his cup of wine and turned to leave the triclinium.

I, once again, made it through an entire evening with the nobles without so much as uttering a single word.

As the nobles began pouring out, I absented myself to my quarters. And there I sat at the foot of my bed and tested the weight of my sword.

As IT TURNS OUT, Scipio was as brilliant a political strategist as he was a military strategist. His simple phrase "who here has received farms" spread like an insulae fire across Rome. By the first week of August, the phrase was indeed scribbled across the oldest temples in the forum, and indeed some even said it was painted on the rostra itself. Perhaps the people weren't howling for Tiberius' blood, but they were certainly howling for answers. Fortunately for the nobles, Tiberius wasn't around to provide them.

It was dreadfully hot that summer, even for Rome. The air was heavy and thick, difficult to breathe, so Scipio and I took to the roof most evenings where it was a bit cooler than indoors. Most of the time we spent in silence. He was an odd fellow, now that I really think about it. He demanded constant companionship, but a silent one. He merely needed to know I was there. And if I'm being honest, if it wasn't me there, I'm certain he would have had another protege to take my place.

It was here that a strange messenger arrived.

"Gerrae, the sun is almost setting," Scipio said, irritated at the disturbance. "If you have a message you can leave it with my doorman."

"I'm sorry, sir, but this message is for Gaius Marius. I was ordered to deliver it into his hands only."

My eyes widened as Scipio and I both stood to our feet.

"Is that so?" Scipio asked with suspicion.

The only person to write me since I had been staying at Scipio's home was my cousin, and she certainly wouldn't have sent an envoy with a toga, or "ordered" him to deliver the letter in any particular fashion.

"Go ahead, boy." Scipio nodded.

I reached forward and accepted the letter, but maintained eye contact with the messenger as I handed it directly to Scipio. Perhaps this was a ruse to drive a wedge between us. I couldn't imagine who might have desired such a thing, but I wasn't going to keep any secrets from my general, and it was important that he knew it. The messenger exhaled and lowered his eyes.

"That's a familiar seal," Scipio said, sliding his thumb under it. He analyzed me with curiosity. "You have no idea what this is?"

"Not at all, general. Nor do I know who that seal belongs to." I felt my heart beat quicken as if I were on trial.

Scipio ripped open the seal and unfolded the scroll.

He had only been reading for a moment when he let his head back and bellowed with laughter.

"It seems my brother by law would like you to attend a dinner at his house this evening."

"What? Let me see that." I took the letter from Scipio as he continued to laugh and pored over the contents. In a few short sentences and elegant penmanship, I had indeed been invited to the Gracchi home. Tiberius' name was signed at the bottom. "I... I..." I looked to Scipio hoping to find the means to explain myself.

"It's alright, lad. I know you've done nothing to betray me."

"The tribune simply wishes to talk," the envoy said, clearly irritated that the contents of the scroll had been shared with Scipio.

"Silence. We're talking," Scipio pointed a finger at the man's chest. "So the bastard must be back in Rome."

"The *tribune* is indeed back in Rome. He arrived early this morning."

"We must have really frightened him then." Scipio grinned.

"Tell your master I decline his offer." I turned again to the envoy.

"Decline? You will certainly go!" Scipio said, his smile evaporating.

"Go, sir?"

"Yes, absolutely."

"He probably wants me to spy on you... learn your next move."

"No doubt he does. But you wouldn't do that. You are loyal aren't you?" Scipio asked.

"Of course, general."

"You wouldn't tell him anything then, would you?"

"No..." I thought about it for a moment. "But he's smarter than me."

"He's not clever enough to break a good man's constitution. He's better at pandering to toothless plebs. And it was such a courteous offer, after all, how could you refuse? He, no doubt, wants to learn my intentions, but perhaps you can discover his in the process."

"I'd rather you not come if you plan on spying on the

tribune," the envoy spoke up, clearly exasperated and fearing the repercussions.

"And what are you going to do about it, boy?" Scipio towered over the envoy like he was a misbehaving soldier in formation. The envoy said nothing.

"If you want me to go, I'll go," I said. There was a part of me that was intrigued, but it was hard to feel that due to the fear that I had somehow been duplicitous. Perhaps my private approval of Tiberius' speeches hadn't been so secret after all. Regardless, I had felt like a no-named entity for some time. Scipio did his best to mention me occasionally in the dinner parties with the nobles, but the majority of the time I remained a silent bystander. Now I was receiving a personal invitation to the infamous tribune's home.

"Of course I want you to go. Change into one of my whitest togas and be on your way. I'm quite interested in hearing what he has to say."

THE ENVOY OFFERED to see me to Tiberius' home, but I declined. I preferred to travel alone and collect my thoughts. As I'm sure you know by our time in Gaul, my sense of direction is impeccable, and I had already memorized the way to the Gracchan domus from our one dinner visit there.

When I arrived, none other than Cornelia greeted me at the door.

"You must be Gaius Marius. It is a pleasure." She held out her hand for me to kiss, which I hurried to do. I was far more nervous talking to Cornelia then I was to speak with Tiberius. Something about noble ladies, I suppose. Now that I think of it, there was something about her that reminds me of my wife Julia. Perhaps it was how elegant, and effortless, her every movement was. "Please, come in." She led the way into the atrium, passing by those ancestral masks on the wall.

"Thank you, ma'am," I said, realizing it was the first thing I had been able to utter.

"Tell my son-in-law that his speech was wonderful. Very well done. I doubt there are any other senators in Rome who would have been capable of turning the people against my son." I couldn't tell if she was being genuine or not, but I couldn't detect any duplicity in her voice.

"I hope it hasn't caused you much trouble, ma'am," I replied, brushing my hand over my hair to ensure it was presentable.

"Not at all. We've had to have a few of our slaves wash the graffiti off our walls a time or two, but that's politics. The people will remember Tiberius' promise, and they will see the marvelous work he has done, in time."

I could find nothing else to say, but fortunately we had arrived in the triclinium, where Tiberius was sitting alone, his eyes locked on the stone bust of his grandfather Scipio Africanus.

"Your guest has arrived, my dear."

Tiberius immediately broke his gaze and stood to his feet.

"Gaius Marius, it's a pleasure to see you again."

"I'll let you two talk." I kissed her hand again and she departed. My heart immediately slowed.

"I was afraid you might not accept my invitation." Tiberius approached and extended his hand. He gripped my forearm firmly, like a man or a soldier, rather than a politician.

"To be honest, Tribune, I almost did not."

"I understand that entirely. My brother-in-law can be a cautious man. I was afraid he would believe I was up to mischief if he heard about my invitation."

"And are you?"

"Am I what?" he asked, gesturing for me to sit on a couch across from his own.

"Up to mischief."

"Not at all," he replied. He didn't seem to be offended by the implications. "I just want to talk."

"About Aemilianus?"

"No. About the legion." That piqued my interest. "I hope you don't mind, but a few other guests will be joining us shortly."

"And who might that be?" I said with a bad taste in my mouth. I might have had conflicting opinions on Tiberius, but I had grown to despise the rabble rousing company he kept. The nobles had made sure of that.

"Greetings, brother," Gaius Gracchus said entering the triclinium with our mutual companion Publius Rutilius Rufus.

"Just these two," Tiberius answered me. "How are you?" He gripped their forearms the way he had mine, and kissed them on either cheek.

"Blessed and healthy." Rufus replied, as stoic then as he is now.

"I'm glad to hear it. Please, sit," Tiberius gestured to two other couches beside ours, but the both of them greeted me before taking their seats.

"I had no notion I'd be seeing you here," Gaius said, a bit more cautious than his brother. He seemed as young as when I last saw him. He now wore the tribune's crest but he still appeared a boy playing at politician.

"I was invited."

"It's good to see you again, old friend." Rufus embraced me firmly. "How is the old general? You're said to be his favorite these days."

"He's blessed and healthy as well."

"And I'm glad to hear that as well," Tiberius said with a nod. "But I did not invite you all here to talk about Scipio. I have no ill will towards the man." He took his seat and made eye contact with me directly. "He was my greatest friend once. When we served in Africa together, we shared a tent. Greatest friend, but also many other things. Brother, father, mentor… and I'd still welcome him in each capacity if he'd have me. But he will not." Tiberius' eyes revealed genuine sadness. I was inclined to trust it, but perhaps it was all for show. "That is not why I've invited you all here this evening, though."

"Why have you invited us, if you don't mind my asking?" Rufus asked, apparently no more informed than I was.

Tiberius stood to his feet and paced the way he had at our first dinner together.

"Are any of you hungry? I could have my cook prepare something."

No one said anything.

"I didn't think so. Soldiers are easily sated, aren't we? And that is precisely why you are all here. I want to talk to you about our men of service. Each of you have served in Rome's most recent war, and as I understand it, each of you has served with distinction. I've heard that you have the admiration and respect of the men. That is why you are here."

Slaves appeared with empty chalices and gracefully poured each of us some of the finest Falernian grape wine.

"Do you hear that?" Tiberius asked. We all fell silent

and perked up our ears, and indeed there was a slight rumble outside the home. Light banging and muffled voices. "Those are retired legionaries. Mother says they've been coming for the past few weeks, every few nights, to shout that I have betrayed them." Tiberius took his seat again and lowered his head. "And that grieves me deeply. I knew when I proposed my legislation that the people who didn't receives farms would become disappointed. I love them, but they are... shortsighted. The soldiers though, those who have sweat and bled for the Republic... I hoped to always have them on my side."

"You do, Tiberius, you just need to speak to them," Gaius Gracchus spoke up, looking up at his older brother with adoration.

"General Aemilianus loves the legionaries too. And he hopes they will always be on *his* side," I said. I was surprised at how forthright I was being, considering the respect I shared for the tribune, but I was cautious lest that fact be made know.

Tiberius nodded and considered my words. "Yes. He absolutely loves the men. And they love him back, as they should. I would never seek to break the bond between legionary and general. That is sacred. But my brother-in-law's first loyalty will always be to the nobility. He believes, as did many of our forefathers, that the future of Rome belongs to the success or failure of Rome's old families. I disagree, but I will never fault him for his conclusion."

I considered replying, but Tiberius' response was so respectful I couldn't bring myself to do so.

He stood again, a man always teeming with passion, his mind producing words quicker than he could say them.

"Many of the men in my position served under the Colors as a means to an end. But I cherished my time in the legion. I remember the nights of stale bread and lukewarm wine with fondness." He looked away and seemed to drift into his memories as the veterans continued to clamor outside. He snapped back to the present, "My mother, virtuous though she is, has always been too protective of her sons. She protected us from the consequences of our actions. Out there, under the standard, I was just a man with a sword."

"Is that why you are at this sad pass? Because you failed to prepare for the consequences of your actions?" Rufus asked, sternly but not with any disrespect. If any man ever embodied the Stoic teaching of Zeno, it was he.

Tiberius smiled sadly and met his eyes. "No. Unfortunately, I learned to anticipate the consequences long ago." The tribune retook his seat and sipped on his wine in silence for a moment. "But the one thing I cannot endure is to lose the respect and love of my brothers in arms. That is why you are here. You have the ear of the men, and I want to hear what it is that they desire. I want you to tell me what they want."

"The veterans are made up of many types of men. They don't all want the same thing," Rufus replied.

"All men want the same thing. On Jupiter's Stone, I believe that. They want less of what they do have and more of what they don't. They want peace. Security. Sustenance they can rely on. A happy wife and healthy children—"

"Well, I'm afraid you'll have a difficult time passing legislation that will make wives happy or children healthy," Rufus interrupted. For a moment I saw rage flash before Tiberius' eyes, but it dissipated before anyone else seemed to notice.

"No. I cannot give them that. I'm not certain even the gods could. But I can give them the land they need to feed their children and earn the living required to buy their wives a seashell necklace."

"If you've already figured it out, why do you need us?" Rufus asked, unaware of the discomfort he was creating.

"*Gerrae*, let the man speak!" Gaius Gracchus shouted.

"It's alright, dear brother. I didn't invite Rufus or Marius here to patronize me. I want to hear what Rome's veterans desire."

"They want their terms of service shortened," I said before I could stop myself. By this time I was very much inclined to remain in silence as I had at Aemilianus' evening gatherings. But it was clear by now that Tiberius hadn't invited me for political intelligence, but to improve the lives of my brothers.

"Is that right?" Tiberius' brows raised. "I knew they desired fewer campaigns, but I didn't know that the length of the campaigns concerned them."

"Our Numantine war veterans had been there for years. Most of them at least. It was a war without end, besieging an impenetrable city belonging to foreigners they couldn't even pronounce the name of. It's not like it was in the old days. That enemy wasn't threatening Roman freedom. Their farms weren't in danger. But they spent four years or more far away from home, away from their wives and newborns, and for what? They returned with no plunder. No glory outside of a triumph. Rome itself is no safer than it was before. It's only her prestige that has increased, not her safety," I blurted out quickly, before I could consider the consequences. I feared for a moment that I had said too much, and that Tiberius would sense that I had supported him all along. But instead he nodded his head and contemplated all I had said.

"And the men don't care about Roman prestige. Why

should they? The only men who benefit are the nobles who take their land and spit on them."

Rufus added, "Marius is right. When we arrived in Spain the legions were utterly unconcerned. They were hardly soldiers by the time we arrived. The only reason they wished for the war to end was because they wished to return home. And if Scipio hadn't arrived, they'd likely still be there."

"Good. Thank you for sharing this." Tiberius tapped his lip and stared at the floor in deep contemplation. Silence fell, and I realized the veterans outside the home had left. "I have four months left in office as tribune. And I vow to you, all three of you, that if it remains within my power to do so, I will pass legislation to shorten the terms of service. I'll put a finite number on it, so that even in a war without end a man can see his children grow up. Will you speak with your compatriots and let them know this?"

Gaius nodded along without hesitation. Rufus considered it but eventually acknowledged his consent. It was a reasonable request, after all.

"I'm still loyal to Scipio Aemilianus," I said. There wasn't a thing Tiberius had said which I disagreed with, and his demeanor had won me more than any of the speeches I had yet witness, but I was still frightened that I might seem dishonest or Janus-faced.

Tiberius took a sip of his wine and then set the cup down. He stood and approached me, and then placed a hand on my shoulder.

"And I wouldn't have invited you here if I believed otherwise. But I do trust that your loyalty to your brothers is higher than to any other, save the gods. If that's the case, all I ask is that you tell them that there is a man in Rome who will do everything in his power to serve them."

And how could I dispute that? At length I nodded my consent.

Before the stillness became uncomfortable, another guest arrived, one with a distinctive foreign element.

"Tribune Gracchus, I come with word from the King of Pergamum," the emissary said in a noticeable eastern accent.

Tiberius seemed as shocked as we were, but his eyes glistened too.

"Excuse me, gentlemen, but I'd best see to this. Gaius, would you see our guests out?"

Tiberius shook my hand once more before I departed, but this time he kissed my cheek as well.

I hurried back to the Domus of Scipio Aemilianus, anxiously crafting what I would tell him when I returned. If he were still alive I'd be too ashamed to say this, but I had to lie to him. He despised Tiberius so deeply that he would have never believed that the man was just inviting me to his home to share a cup of wine and talk about how he might serve Rome's veterans better.

Instead, I would tell him that the Tribune had attempted to sway me to his cause, and that I had resisted.

One thing was certain though, I wasn't going to be mentioning the emissary from Pergamum. That spelled trouble and I wanted nothing to do with it.

Scipio believed and approved of the version of events that I recited for him. I was ashamed, and perhaps still am, that I was forced to lie to my mentor. But one thing I had already learned about politics was that there were narratives at play here: bad men versus good men, demagogues versus the defenders of the constitution... and it always behooves a man to play to those narratives. Only when one has achieved power can you abandon them. And then perhaps you become a narrative yourself.

A few weeks passed before any news came of that emissary from Pergamum, and I eventually believed it was unimportant. Tiberius' father was a man of incredible influence and prestige, a patron of many foreign nations before he died, although he died young. Perhaps it was a friendly gesture from a foreign king to the son of a man who had protected him.

This naive idea was proven wrong early one morning when Aemilianus and I were working in his tablinum.

Marcus Octavius burst in and said he needed to speak with Scipio, the door guard following behind him, fearful he might be punished for the intrusion. The man might have been utterly bested by Tiberius on the rostra, but he was no fool. He wouldn't have disturbed a man like Scipio Aemilianus unless it was necessary.

"What is it? What's wrong?" Scipio asked, sensing the same thing I was.

"Dismiss your dogs," he said gesturing to the slaves in the room, and perhaps to me. Scipio flicked his wrist and everyone departed but the three of us. I wasn't going to leave until I was expressly told to do so. Octavius eyed me with suspicion but I didn't budge and neither did Scipio, so he proceeded.

"The king of Pergamum has died. And he has left his kingdom to the people of Rome."

Scipio looked at me with raised brows and nodded his head.

"Then why do you look so glum and gloomy? This is

great news! That's the easiest territory Rome has ever conquered, is it not?" the general asked.

"Sir." Octavius kneeled and bowed his head as if he were standing before a king.

"Out with it," Scipio said, standing to his feet.

"The emissary is staying in the home of Tiberius Gracchus."

Nothing else needed to be said.

Aemilianus breathed heavily.

"And who exactly did his will designate as the ruler of his kingdom?" he asked, his brows furrowed and lips pursed.

"The *people* of Rome."

It was several weeks before any kind of announcement was made public. As soon as word reached Aemilianus that Tiberius was taking the rostra, we hurried to the forum without waiting for any kind of cortege to form.

"The King of Pergamum, Attalus III, has left his kingdom to you, the people!" Tiberius was shouting from the rostra by the time we arrived. Scipio didn't delay. He didn't stop to issue instruction to myself or the other followers present.

"The hero of the people!" Tiberius shouted. And he was the first to applaud the general. I've always wondered if anyone would have clapped if Tiberius hadn't done so himself. How fickle the people have always been!

I had been present to witness how they had turned on him. But the moment their hero took to the rostra, they were silenced into submission. Silent, that is, until Tiberius gave them license to do otherwise.

"Would you like to address the people?" Tiberius asked, and again I was conflicted. It did seem like he was setting a trap, but perhaps that was simply the kind of man Tiberius Gracchus was. He didn't appear duplicitous, even when giving the floor to his enemies.

"I've now had a chance to study the will of the king of Pergamum. And he did not leave his kingdom to the people, but to the SPQR, the Senate and Populace of Rome!" The people gasped and looked to Tiberius for an answer. As far as I knew, Aemilianus had never gazed upon that will, even for a brief moment. But it didn't matter. All he had to do was suggest that Tiberius was taking liberties with the law, and his enemy was under suspicion.

"Do you not see, citizens, what is happening?" Tiberius said, gesturing to his brother-in-law with a smile and a shake of the head. "This is the man who did everything within his power to turn you against me. And why? Because I did not provide farms fast enough. What deception! What trickery! This is the same man who opposed my measures in the first place! And he considers himself a member of the same faction which has made my measures a nightmare to carry out from it's very conception!" Tiberius cried. And this time, when the people gasped it was not out of surprise, but out of anger. Anger, fury, that their famed hero had betrayed them.

"I simply wish to uphold the law," Scipio said, refusing to take the bait of his foe.

"You do? You do? Well isn't that interesting! Because the oldest mandate in the state is that land disputes belong to the people! And yet here you stand, opposing the will of the people, attempting to leverage your well-earned glory in battle to benefit not the soldiers who served under you, but the men who have always lorded over you!"

The plebeians cried out. Aemilianus tried to respond but his words were drowned out by the mob.

"And this is the man who cried 'who among you has received a farm' but if it wasn't for the nobles opposing me, I would have received, a thousand fold, the resources necessary to give each and every one of you a parcel of land and the resources to maintain it!" Tiberius cried.

I wasn't sure if this was true. But it didn't matter. This was Tiberius' masterstroke. The people, who had so recently clamored for answers, would never again cry at his doorstep. If they didn't receive farms it wasn't because Tiberius was fooling them, it was because nobles like Scipio were blocking his endeavors.

Once again he proved to be just a bit more clever than they were.

"And let me tell you what the patricians are really waiting for!" Tiberius shouted. Scipio stepped back and allowed his enemy to continue. Perhaps he was just as curious about what the tribune might say as the rest of us were. "They want to wait out my term office. They think if they can hold off until December they can purchase enough tribunes with purses of gold coins that they'll reclaim what *you* have taken from them." It was a masterful job, to say "you" rather than "I", but even at the time, standing at the foot of the rostra, I could find no internal arguments to disagree with him.

"But don't let them, my people! Don't let them! You have taken only what you deserve by birthright as Roman citizens. You have passed the measures I've proposed. And now that the gods have revealed a way to not only fund these measures but also give land to all our deserving veterans, how can the senate try to block them?" And now I felt guilty. I was careful not to meet Scipio's gaze, but thankfully it was cast out into the nameless multitude. "They can only block it if they turn you against me! But you know that I have ever stood for the rights of the people, and her veterans."

The look on Scipio's face revealed that he understood what was happening. He had walked into a trap and he was aware of it.

"Citizens, you must desire truth rather than pandering speeches!" Scipio cried. But I only heard it because I was so close to the rostra. The majority were unlikely to hear it over the tumult.

"And now I'd like to announce the most important thing on my agenda," Tiberius said, and his voice was easy to hear over the tumult, no matter how loud it became. "I will be running for tribune again."

The people gasped and then fell silent.

"I have much more to do. Things I have always wanted to do, but have never been able to accomplish. Why? Because of fine noblemen like this one!" He shouted out to the crowd but pointed directly at Scipio. "The first thing I will do is shorten the term of service for all eligible legionaries." You already know I felt a supreme guilt at this juncture. I had lied to Scipio about my meeting with the tribune, and for good reason. Had I known that he would use what I had told him to earn another tribuneship, I would have kept my mouth shut.

"And I will also use the coffers of the deceased king of Pergamum to fund the expansion of our farmland, as well as give this new land to our most deserving citizens: the veterans who have bled for our sovereignty!"

Needless to say, I never again attended a dinner at Tiberius' home. But I was never again invited.

Scipio and I burst into his Domus, both of us in a sweat. I rushed to my room and grabbed my sword, clutching it in my arms as if it would give me strength.

"Marius!" Scipio demanded my presence so I hurried back out into the atrium, unaware that I had brought my sword with me.

He was knelt over the *impluvium* and splashing water over his head, breathing heavily. He looked up at my, water dripping over his rapidly blinking eyes, "What has happened?" He asked. And I was not sure if the question was rhetorical.

Before I was forced to respond, a tumult sounded from the entryway and the doorman screamed.

Instinct took over and I grabbed the hilt of my sword, but of course it was Laelius and Octavius.

"What has happened?" Octavius shouted. Clearly he didn't know either. "What are we to do now?" He cried.

"We nearly got lynched in the street trying to get here! That demagogue has the entire city on the verge of a revolt!" Laelius bellowed.

Scipio shook his head rapidly and slapped the water like a child.

"You bloody fools! If I knew how to beat the man I would have done so already!" He gritted his teeth and the veins in his neck and forehead bulged. I had never seen him so ill composed.

"We have to do something though," Octavius said sheepishly.

Before Scipio could scream any further, the doors burst open again, and in stormed the pontifex maximus.

"Look what you have done!" Nasica roared without

hesitation. "This is your fault, Aemilianus!" His toga was disheveled, and he moved quicker than I had ever seen him. His beady little eyes were squinted in fury, and he pointed those bony fingers directly at Aemilianus' chest.

Given the crazed look in Aemilianus' eye, I feared his patience with his cousin might finally be at in end. So before the high priest could reach my general, I stepped in his way, palm gripped on my hilt.

He looked up at me in shock and disgust, but was wise enough not to step any closer.

"Get out! Get out! All of you! You were not invited to my home, now get out!" Aemilianus roared, thrashing his arms in the water wildly.

Nasica didn't test his luck by pushing past me, but he stepped aside so that he could force his cousin to meet his eyes.

"We have to kill him, Aemilianus! We have to kill him now before it's too late. Buy off his cook to poison him, or bribe a slave to smother him in his sleep."

"Get out! None of you are welcome here now. Leave my home!" Scipio roared clutching his fists. I was thankful that I had the sword instead of he.

"Are you with me, Aemilianus? He was brother to you once. I need to know that you are with me. We have to kill him."

"Out!"

Octavius and Laelius both hesitated for a moment, both bewildered and terrified by the outburst of their leader. But eventually they turned and hurried for the door.

Nasica refused to budge.

"I need to know that you are with me, Aemilianus. Tell me that you know he has to die. And tell me now. Say that you'll support me in this."

Aemilianus' fists clinched until the knuckles were white, and he brought one trembling to his lips.

"I said out!"

"All you need to say is that you are with me, Aemilianus. Say you want him dead and I'll take care of the rest. Say it. Tell me. Say it now!"

"Get out, cousin, I beg you!"

"Say it, Aemilianus. Or were you with the tribune all along?"

Before I could consider the implications or consequences, I brandished my sword and pointed it at Nasica. The tip of it gleamed in the candle light of Aemilianus' masks, not but a few inches from Nasica's chest.

Nasica was flabbergasted. "You cannot lay a hand on the high priest!"

"I would *never* lay a *finger* on the high priest," I said, walked closer to him and forcing him to step backwards towards the exit. "But my sword here, see, she doesn't have the same scruples. She's killed better men then you, and she's thirsty from seeing so much action without drawing blood." I felt my teeth gritting and a snarl develop across my face.

I continued to back him further away from Aemilianus, and closer to the door.

"Cousin, call off this mad dog before I have him put down!" Nasica shouted, but the tone of his voice had changed drastically. He did his best to appear as haughty as he was accustomed to being, but I could see his thin lips trembling with fear.

Aemilianus said nothing. I could feel his eyes on us, but I took his silence for compliance. So I pushed the tip of my sword further still, until it hovered an inch from the high priest's sternum.

I hadn't realized until then that I had wanted to kill him since the very beginning. Perhaps it was misplaced anger. Maybe I wanted to point my sword at Tiberius instead. But it was Nasica here now. And if he made one false move, I would have damned my soul to eternal punishment and cast my political career into oblivion. I would have killed him. Without pause.

"My general says you need to leave. And leave you shall. I won't hurt you, high priest, but my sword is *loyal* to Scipio Aemilianus."

He finally accepted that Aemilianus wasn't going to intervene.

"I'm going to have you crucified for this, boy." He straightened his shoulders and tried his best to appear noble. But no matter how hard he tried he couldn't prevent the quiver of his voice.

"No you aren't. The moment you say a word about this... to your wife, to your mistress, to your priests... I will hear of it," I fully extended my arm, forcing him to jump back, "and if I do hear of it, I will tell the whole world that you plan to have a tribune of the Roman Republic assassinated in the most cowardly and despicable manner."

Nasica locked eyes with Aemilianus and nodded to the masks on his wall.

"If you ever want to find your face up there with our ancestors, you need to act. These were men of force and probity... they would be disappointed." To my chagrin, Aemilianus said nothing in return, still knelt silently with water dripping from his chin.

Finally, to my relief, Nasica turned and took long strides to the door. He paused before he exited, however, and lifted his left arm to me with both his little and forefinger extended.

"I curse you, in the name of all the gods, I curse you. To a life of misery and suffering. Even when you believe you have reached the pinnacle of your pathetic life, you will be cast down, spat out by the gods. You will taste bitterness and despair; you will drink your own tears. And you will die alone. No progeny will bear your name."

With that, he hurried through the door.

I did not turn to Scipio and he didn't ask me any questions. I sheathed my gladius and hurried to my quarters, where I would lie awake all night, thinking about the high priest's curse.

IN THE MORNING, I continued to lie in bed for some time. Even after the sun began to pour in under the door to my room, I desired some modicum of rest. I had a long day of travel ahead, after all.

For I had made up my mind. I was going to leave. Rome was no place for me, after all. Perhaps I was accustomed to the simple life of being a debauched farmer's son. Perhaps I wasn't intelligent or discerning enough for politics. Even then, after Tiberius had used our friendly dinner to announce that he would continue his reign over Rome, I did not hate the man. I was hurt, certainly. But that didn't mean I disapproved of his politics. And if he could actually shorten the term of military service for my brothers, I hoped he would win.

But I had done enough to harm my general. Not only had I divulged information which aided his political opponent, I had threatened his cousin at sword point within the walls of his very home. Depending how one looks at it, I had even implicated him in a conspiracy to murder the pontifex maximus of Rome.

There was no going back. I couldn't continue to dine with Scipio and his associates and listen to them ramble on about the mos maiorum and the republic and Tiberius' power. I couldn't sit with him in silence on the rooftops, or share stories about our time in Spain together.

When at last I resigned to the fact that Somnus the god of sleep wouldn't be visiting me that morning, I rolled out of bed and gathered what little belonged to me.

I exited my room to find Scipio's domus functioning as it always was. The clients were waiting outside the front door, and Scipio's doorman was escorting each one by one to see their patron. It was as if the man hadn't been splashing around in a pool of water the night before or he hadn't witnessed a farm-hand threaten the life of his cousin.

I made my way into his tablinum where Scipio was seeing each of his clients, seated behind a large desk in a backless chair. I kept my eyes low, ashamed, for I had attended each of Scipio's morning levies since I had begun to stay in his home, occasionally taking notes, other times standing as a living statue of Scipio's love for the veterans.

Even while my gaze was cast at the mosaic on the floor, I could feel the general's eyes on me.

"I will have the matter looked into immediately, Flavius. If you'll excuse me," Scipio gestured for the door.

"Yes, pater... it's just that these thieves have been taking my cattle. Cattle that are earmarked with my brand. It's destroying my way of life and—"

"I said I would have the matter looked into, Flavius. And I will." Scipio's slave began to escort his client to the door. "Cleon, give the good farmer Flavius 50 denarii. And tell my next client to wait until I am finished speaking with Marius," Scipio addressed his slave.

I took that as my sign to look up and meet the gaze of my general.

"You're leaving then?" Scipio asked. He must have noticed the traveling attire.

"I think it would be best, sir. I'm not cut out for this life, it seems."

"Well that's a shame." He exhaled, looked down, and shuck his head. "I think last night showed that you have the ingredients to be a wonderful politician... the kind Rome needs."

I looked up, bristling from the compliment but unaware how I had earned it.

"Your cousin will seek revenge. And I'd rather not start my career by spreading gossip about the high priest."

"He won't do a thing." Scipio shuck his head and waved a hand derisively. "He wouldn't want the republic to know how easily he was backed down. Or, more importantly, that a man can raise a sword against the high priest and not be struck down by the gods."

"Cursed by a high priest. That really is something. Not many men my age can say they've ever accomplished something like that." We both laughed. But then silence followed. "I should be going then," I said. And this time I did not phrase it as a question. Each time I had mentioned leaving, Scipio was able to talk me out of it in the past. This time was different. There was no going back, for obvious reasons.

"You're leaving then?"

"I think it's best that I do."

"Well, that's such a shame. Especially considering what I was able to do for you this morning."

I was almost finished rehearsing the final goodbyes in my mind when he said this. But that forced me to pause.

"What have you done for me this morning?"

"I was able to do something, quite incredible, for you this morning. While you were sleeping in, I was forging the path of your career." He locked his eyes with mine.

"I wasn't sleeping, general. I was thinking about that curse."

He laughed.

"I wouldn't worry too much about it. He didn't sacrifice an animal on it, did he? And he's too miserly to purchase one at his own expense. So I trust you'll be safe. He's about as pious as that Spanish trollop you used to lie with, so I'm not sure the gods hear his cries any clearer than they hear the rest."

I smiled uncomfortably and waited for him to continue, but he didn't.

"What did you accomplish, sir?"

"Oh, that's right." He knew he had my attention and he did his best to take advantage of that. He stood, clasped his arms behind his back, and stared at the statue of his adoptive grandfather Scipio Africanus. "As of this morning, I've secured you a position as military tribune on the staff of my colleague Metellus. He's taking a force to the Gymnesian Islands for conquest. And this could be the beginning of a bright future for you, young man."

I paused for some time, allowing the words to set in. It didn't seem believable. I could almost feel the sword at my hip glistening at the opportunity to seek further glory.

"You did this, sir?"

"I did." Scipio turned to me again and analyzed my reaction. "Marius, let me be clear with you. Let me tell you something about myself. I do not trust anyone. Not a single man in Rome holds my trust... save those who have shed blood for me. I only trust a man once I've seen his resolve tested. Once I've seen a spear at his throat. And when he is loyal then, I'll give him all the trust I can muster in my old embittered heart. I don't trust Laelius, Octavius, or my cousin Nasica. Why? Well... I haven't seen them shed blood for me and stand firm. But you have." Aemilianus touched the face of Africanus' bust and then reclaimed his seat.

"I don't trust anyone, Marius. Not even my wife. And, if I'm not wrong... and I am very rarely wrong... she would gladly open up the doors to my enemies to have them slaughter me in my sleep. I have not given you free lodgings and fine foods for nearly a year because I enjoy your company, although I do. I needed a protector. And whether you know it or not, my would-be enemies fear you. No one would try to "smother me in my sleep" or "bribe my cook" when the vicious Gaius Marius is within my home." He let his head back and bellowed with laughter. There were many facets to Scipio that I was beginning to see that I had not noticed previously.

"I think I understand, general," I said, with a smile and a nod of the head.

Then he straightened up and his face became as serious as a bust of Mars.

"And that's why I need you to remain here. Until five days before the Ides of December, the election of the tribunes of the people. If you'll remain here with me, I'll ensure you have a position on the most lucrative campaign Rome has seen in a hundred years. I need you to ensure I remain safe within my own home."

I shook my head, disagreeing, but I didn't know what exactly I was disagreeing with.

"Sir, Sempronia would never—"

"Sempronia would sooner see me eaten by wolves than have a child with me. And Tiberius' tactics have become increasingly deceptive."

"Sir," I said, instantly kneeling and lowering my head. I felt my heart thud against my chest as I prepared to say what I must. "I was the one who told Tiberius that the soldiers wished to see their length of service shorten. If I hadn't said that he might not have had the platform to run for tribune again."

"Rise, Marius," he said, irritated. "That's nonsense. My brother by law is an intelligent man. He likely knew this already."

"But he seemed surprised. Stunned by that information." I stood to my feet again, but couldn't meet his gaze, now that he knew the truth.

"Of course that's the way he desired to seem. He's a great actor, my brother by law. Better than any pantomime in the forum. But he knew this already or would have discovered it on his own. He simply wanted you to feel responsible for it so that he could drive you away from me. He wanted to drive a wedge between us. And perhaps when you left, he would have been able to send his henchmen in to kill me."

"General... would he really do this?" I asked, deeply hurt. Scipio looked at me with wet, sad eyes.

"The people once loved me as they loved Romulus. I can't set bounds on whom Tiberius can and can't take away from me."

I'm certain you already know what I did. I wasn't certain the life of a politician was the one for me, especially considering the current political climate. I knew that the returning to my family farm wasn't an option. The legion was the only place I belonged. It was the only place my sword and I would ever feel at home.

I would miss my daughter, to be certain. But what kind of father would she really want to have? The kind who ran away from his destiny, a grown man who continues to live under the thumb of his oppressive father? Or a conquering hero, a military tribune no less?

So, it was here that I found myself with Aemilianus, ascending the steps of the senate house. It was six days before the Ides of December, the day before the elections, and I hoped this would be the last time I'd be required to come here for the foreseeable future.

"Bring your sword," Scipio had told me as his slaves wrapped his toga and shawl around him. "We might need it."

The situation hadn't calmed any over the past few months. Indeed, as the autumn turned to winter, the political affairs in Rome became worse.

Tiberius refused to leave Rome again. He told the people that if they wanted to see all of his measures be brought to fruition, they would need to reelect him. He also cited the fact that if he left the nobles would ensure he was defeated as another reason for his presence, an observation that was no doubt true.

The number of Tiberius' armed supporters continued to grow. By now he had amassed a small army. He spoke from the rostra about how this was necessary to ensure his safety. Some of the nobles claimed he was cracking, growing weak and paranoid, not to mention tyrannical. But he had reason to suspect that his life was in danger. Nasica wasn't the only man to whisper his desire to have Tiberius murdered.

People from all over Italy came and set up tents outside the tribune's home on the Palatine to protect him. Some ignored the cold and slept under the stars, with daggers at their sides. Some said they had guard shifts scheduled for days in advance, which made me wonder if some of these supporters were once Scipio's veterans.

Today was the last day the nobles could mount a defense against Tiberius. If they wished to ban him from running for tribune again, they would have to do so today. The following morning would see the voting booths set out and citizens from all over Italy would gather to ensure their voice was heard. Those men who had received farms, the same ones who hadn't been there to protect Tiberius when Aemilianus said "who has received farms", were already flocking into the city as a demonstration of their support.

And while Tiberius' support with the people reached its ultimate height, the nobles remained fractured.

After Tiberius announced that he would be running for reelection, all his support within the senate house vanished. The Claudians, his in-laws, turned their back on him without question. Even his father in law, who had benefited as much as any man from Tiberius' reforms, seemed to disappear from his side at the assemblies.

So all the nobles wished to see Tiberius defeated. But how they planned to do so was another matter. The Scipiones distrusted the Claudians because they had supported Tiberius for so long. The Fabians distrusted anyone outside their own faction. The Scipiones were torn for reasons that only I knew. Since I had marched Nasica out at sword point, Aemilianus and his cousin had barely been on

speaking terms, only when necessary and to keep up political appearances.

I STOPPED AS ALWAYS behind the partition rope outside the
entry to the Temple of Concord, where the senate would be
meeting that day, this time with a sword concealed beneath
my heaviest wool cloak. It was quite ironic that we were
meeting at the Temple of Concord that day, as the goddess
of peace herself would be overseeing a debate that was
anything but peaceful.

My general Aemilianus continued on inside. When he
reached the doors, he turned and looked me in the eye.

"Don't let anyone enter." He was barely audible but I
could read his lips. I gave him a nod as he turned and found
his seat beside his cousin and Gaius Laelius.

I saw Tiberius sitting along with the other tribunes on a
bench at the foot of the stands. He neither talked to those
around him nor fidgeted uncomfortably. His eyes were fixed
ahead, once again, like the statues of him that would soon be
destroyed.

I tried to warm my hands as I waited. It was frightfully
cold that winter, a white gloss of frost covering the colonnades of the temple. The breath of those gathered around
me created such a visible steam it appeared a fire was
burning.

And behind me, the masses were growing even larger. It
appeared all of Rome had come out, despite the frost, to
hear whether the famous tribune would be denied his
request of another election.

They were silent enough that even those farthest away

were able to hear the booming voice of the consul as he began.

"Conscript Fathers, I will begin without hesitation. You all know why we are here. All other discussions will be tabled until a time when the future of our Republic isn't at stake," Consul Mucius Scaevola said, his voice teeming on rage. Everyone seemed to forget that Scaevola was one of the Claudians who was so recently numbered amongst the tribune's most vehement supporters. "And the fact that this *tribune*, has the insolence to show his face within this august body even as he spits on everything we represent, should show you what kind of man we're dealing with!"

The senators stomped their feet in agreement, and the people outside moaned and shook their heads.

Tiberius' eyes followed the consul's gesticulation with intense curiosity, and nothing more.

"I move that Tiberius Gracchus be banned from running for reelection, on the grounds that tribunes have never be allowed to run for two years in a row. But I'm certain, as always, that our young revolutionary will have an answer for breaking the law under the guise of benevolence."

He pointed at Tiberius, challenging him to stand and defend himself. But Tiberius didn't take the bait.

"And unless our seniors would like to speak against him, I give the floor to this rebel to speak for himself."

No one stood, not even Nasica. I believe everyone was anxious to hear what the tribune would say next.

Tiberius, at length, stood to his feet, having waited a respectful amount of time to ensure his betters did not wish to speak before him.

He stood still, his head high, his judging eyes scanning

around the room at the faces of those who had betrayed him and those who had detested him from the beginning.

"What's he saying?" some whispered.

"He's not saying anything," others answered them correctly.

He waited until all was silent, from the balcony of the senate house to the farthest man in the gathering. The tension was as thick as the wool cloak wrapped over my shoulders.

"Conscript Fathers, I have come here today not as a challenge to any of you, but to show you that I am ever a member of this august body. Even when I have circumvented the traditional means of political procedure, I did that out of respect for this body, and ultimately out of love for Rome." This sent all of the senators to their feet, pointing at Tiberius with the left hands and each shouting over the other. Again, he waited for total silence. "I simply have the foresight that many of you are unwilling to accept." The roars began again, even louder this time.

"Who do you think you are?" Nasica screamed over the tumult. Tiberius turned to where the high priest stood in the stands, and smiled.

"I was under the impression that I had the floor, pontifex maximus." The nobles reclaimed their seats, and the revolutionary continued. "You say it is illegal for me to run for tribune again. It seems it is only necessary for a man to follow the laws when it serves your interests, noblemen. For was it not our great hero, Scipio Aemilianus, who ran two consecutive consulships?" he asked. None stood to their feet this time. "And at the time it was said this this break with traditional procedure was necessary for the welfare of the state. And here again, I say my reelection is necessary for the good of the Roman people." The jeering began again, but this time Tiberius spoke over them, and his words were still heard. "Because the people are not crying out for fair elections! They cry out for land! They cry out for jobs, shortened service, and clean water! They cry out for a man who will serve their interests! And who will deny the cry of the people?"

Before I could tell what was happening, armed men pushed by on either side of me. I thought for a moment they were storming the senate house. I grabbed the hilt of my sword, but didn't brandish it when I saw that they all stopped at the precipice of the rope partition, their hands clutched tightly around the exposed clubs and daggers at their hips. I thought about stabbing one of them in the back, but I would have been swallowed up before I draw my sword. I was outnumbered by a dozen or more.

They stood in waiting. And the moment the senators cut their gaze to the men at the door, they fell silent.

"I ask again, who will deny the people?" Tiberius' voice was barely above a whisper now, but each man heard it. "Then the matter is settled. I will stand for tribune tomorrow. And the cry of the people will be heard, one way or the other." With that, Tiberius adjusted his toga and stepped out into the cold.

Immediately the armed men at the rope partition retreated into the crowds and disappeared. Tiberius waited outside the door as the senators piled out, standing by pleasantly as if he were strolling in the forum. He waited for anyone willing to stop by and shake his hand, but no one came. And I don't think he ever believed they would. I'm not sure if anyone else could see, but I could see several men of his regime standing behind him with eyes on the tribune, ready to pounce if any of the nobles tried something foolish.

Scipio exited along with many of the other senators, none of whom were talking.

"Let's go home," he said, his voice low and his face downcast, as he approached. He wouldn't be standing by to banter with the other nobles today. He was all out of things to say.

"Brother," Tiberius approach behind him. To my surprise, Scipio didn't seem shocked to find him there. "Are you not going to congratulate me?"

"I am so sorry, Tiberius." Scipio looked down and shook his head. I believe his eyes shimmered with tears, but perhaps it was just the cold. "I have failed you. I was supposed to raise you to be a great man, the man who might take my place in the senate house one day. But I have failed you."

Tiberius placed a hand on Scipio's shoulder, and his henchmen stepped a bit closer.

"You have never failed me, Scipio Aemilianus. You have been faithful and good to me." He seemed to have changed his tone from the last time they met, when he clamored that Scipio had betrayed him in the senate house while he was still fighting in Numantia.

"Why did it have to be you, Tiberius? You could have risen to the pinnacle of Roman power. You could have been consul. You had the love of the people, the support of the nobles, and clients in every corner of the Republic. Why did you have to be the one to throw away your career so foolishly?"

The two men looked at each other, both with sadness and remorse in their eyes. And I couldn't believe what I was seeing with mine. The two spoke together as if one stricken with a terminal illness. And perhaps that's what they both thought about each other.

Neither cursed or raised their voices. It was as if the die had been cast, both were resigned to fate now. And there was nothing either of them could do to go back.

"Because I had the love of the people, the support of the nobles, and clients in every corner of the Republic. That is why it had to be me, brother. It had to be me. No one else could do what I have done. It would have been political suicide."

Scipio's face twisted in agony for a moment, and I couldn't tell if he was about to retch, or if he was about to burst into tears.

"You have committed political suicide, Tiberius." He shook his head sadly as he pointed back into the emptying halls of the senate house, where Tiberius had shown his most recent display of revolution.

Tiberius smiled sadly and brushed back a boyish curl from his forehead with the back of his thumb. "I died a long time ago in Numantia, Scipio. I thought you knew that." He leaned forward and kissed Scipio on the cheek, and squeezed his arm before turning to leave with his mob. Scipio turned and left with myself and the remainder of his clients trailing behind him.

The two men would never speak to each other again.

"Wake up! Wake up!"

I was praying at the altar to the household gods when the voice rang throughout Aemilianus' atrium. I sprang to my feet and grabbed my sword. Just as I made it to the atrium, Scipio arrived as well, his night clothes still wrapped around his shoulders.

The intruder continued screaming until he saw Scipio

running down the stairs towards him. And from the look on his face, he had woken the wrong man.

"No, no, it's the Pontifex Maximus sent me, see," the man said, still panting heavily. As soon as Scipio halted his advance, he leaned over and put his hands on his knees, chest heaving.

"What is the meaning of this? Speak. The sun hasn't yet risen."

"The whole city's gone bloody mad. Tiberius and his supporters went to the forum this morning to pass legislation to legitimize his running for election... bastard knew we'd have him arraigned for it one day," the courier said with a smile, revealing a few missing teeth.

In a few hours, the vote for tribune would be under way. Tiberius must have decided to sneak one final piece of legislation into law to cap off his revolutionary first year as tribune. One could only imagine what might come in the following year if he were reelected.

"And this has caused the city to go mad?" Scipio asked, a slight glimmer of hope in his eye. Perhaps the people had finally caught on to Tiberius' measures and turned against him. Perhaps this would be enough for Tiberius to see reason and stop what he was doing.

"You bet. The nobles caught wind of it, see, and they came out in droves and started pushing through the crowd. A whole uproar, bang, and everybody is fighting. There's some dead now, to be certain."

"Damnit!" Scipio roared. He placed his hands on his hips, pursed his lips and began breathing as heavily as the courier. "Marius gather your things. We need to leave."

"I'll rally your clients," I said, shifting on my heels and heading back to grab my toga.

"No. I won't be going as a senator today."

THE TWO OF us sprinted down from his house on the Palatine, alone. I had my sword, and Scipio had a hooded cloak pulled low over his eyes. What madness could possess a man to run into a fray like this without more protection? I assume his best protection was anonymity though. If he wasn't a noble, he didn't have to fear the wrath of the people. Probably.

An orange sun poked out behind foreboding grey clouds in the east, illuminating the layer of frost on the tops of the temples. Even before we reached the Capitoline hill, we could hear shouting. Noise travels in Rome, as I'm sure you'll come to realize.

And Scipio led me directly towards the chaos.

"You've got your sword?" Scipio was sucking wind, but moving faster than a man his age should be able to.

"Of course."

"I pray we won't have to use it."

We took an alleyway behind a temple to Proserpina and circumvented some of the crowds. As we exited into the forum, we were surrounded by chaos.

In the confusion it was too difficult to make sense of what was happening. The sickening thud of club against flesh rang out and echoed in the temples and empty workshops, followed by the screams and curses of a multitude.

Scipio stood as frozen as the tops of the temples. He didn't possess the means necessary to do a damn thing about the bedlam around us.

"What do you want me to do, general?" I asked, pulling my sword from her scabbard, just enough so he could see the steel glimmering in the morning sun.

"Nothing. Put that away." His gaze was locked across

the forum. As my eyes adjusted to the darkness, I could now see what it was he was looking at. His brother in law stood atop the rostra shouting and gesticulating wildly.

"He's encouraging them to fight," I said, stunned and hurt.

"No. He's calling for them to stop. We must rally the Senate."

"How, sir?" I asked, shaking my head as if to decline the ridiculous suggestion.

I turned my gaze to the rostra again, where Tiberius stood with his armed men behind him, dozens of others attempting to clamor up to him as well. Whether they were friend or foe to the tribune, I couldn't tell.

"It's ancient custom. When there is danger within the city walls, all senators are to meet at the temple of Fides. That is, if they aren't too busy butchering their own people." He sprinted off through the chaos, his cape flapping behind.

Scipio and I were among the first to arrive.

At first I stopped before the entrance, as I was used to doing.

"Come on then. If senators are willing to butcher the people some of them are certainly willing to kill me. I need you to protect me with that sword arm, damnit."

Turtledoves, the symbol of Fides, were etched into every chair within the room, and a large one adorned the alter at the front. So peaceful. Such sharp contrast to the chaos outside.

But I had little time to admire them before there were droves of senators pushing into the ancient temple. Some were in togas, others in their night clothes, others in old tunics or cloaks. Some of them, presumably the purveyors of this morning's violence, had blacked eyes or bloody noses that dripped and stained the cloth. This wasn't such an august looking body when it wasn't powdered and adorned with lavender scented togas.

And they did not come quietly. Most were screaming as loudly as they could about some injustice or another they had encountered on their way there. When the disorganized senate had arrived in enough numbers, Nasica demanded the floor. For some time, the floor wasn't going to be any one man's in particular, as they continued to rage and point fingers at one another for who was the cause of this.

"He was asking for a crown! I saw him, he was asking for a crown!" One of the junior senators shouted, tapping his head as an imitation of the tribune's actions. At the mention of crown, as with anything concerning regency, the entire senate erupted, but this time with a unified voice.

"He was signaling to his people that he was in danger." Scipio's commanding voice rose above the general tumult.

"Whose side are you on?" Some shouted.

"His people? They're our people!" Others joined in.

Aemilianus stood his ground but I stepped in closer, my hand clutched on the hilt of my gladius. No one seemed to notice that I didn't belong there. In fact they didn't seem to notice me at all. They were prepared to rip Scipio Aemilianus to shreds if he so much as insinuated his loyalties lay with Tiberius. Hero or not. Consular or not.

"Traitor!" Some of the senators shouted, but Nasica wailed until they gave him the floor.

"The time has come for action. Senators of Rome, we must act! This man has now caused bloodshed in Rome, the most treacherous thing a Roman can do. He must die!" The senators erupted in applause.

Aemilianus stood by watching, stunned and silent, at a loss for what he might say to speak sense to them. He couldn't speak reason to his brother by law, he couldn't now speak reason to the senate.

"I now call upon, as pontifex maximus, the presiding Consul Mucius Scaevola, to take up arms and defend the state." Nasica approached the Consul and placed a hand on his shoulder. "Your Republic needs you."

The consul seemed to consider it.

"No. I will not."

The senate roared their disapproval.

"I will not be the first to shed blood in my own city!" the consul cried out.

"They shed blood first!" The senators implored.

"All my reports indicate that the people gathered in a lawful assembly this morning!" He attempted to shout over the tumult, but I only heard him because I was nearby.

"Consul, he has shed blood. He has asked for a crown. Every ancient dictate that this Republic is built upon demands that he pay with his blood!" Nasica shouted, his bony fingers digging into the consul's shoulder.

"I will not permit any freeman be killed without a trial and a sentencing. I will not!" I thought for a moment that I would have to step in for the defense of a Roman consul at that point, but Nasica calmed the men around him.

"Since the consul doesn't hold the safety of the commonwealth in higher regard than his own, I will lead you!" Nasica roared as the senate fell to silence. "I will lead you to kill the tyrant! Let every man who values liberty and will stand in defense of our laws, follow me!"

The cry of the senators rose up and echoed throughout

the halls of the Temple of Fides. The turtledoves watched silently.

"Let's free our country!" he cried out. And at this, chaos broke out around us. The senators rushed to smash the tables and benches stationed around us, taking up the broken limbs as clubs.

Nasica approached his cousin. He wore a snarl across his face, one I hadn't seen the likes of before, but I've seen many a times upon the face of an arrogant noble.

"You told me once that we had grown complacent, that we had not done anything. Well now, I *will* do something, cousin. *I* will make our ancestors proud." With that, he departed and the angry horde of senators followed after him.

I felt the outrageous impulse to cut them all down. And I still believe if Scipio had given me so much as a nod of the head, I would have. I was the only one, after all, with a sword. Or military training for that matter.

But Scipio said nothing.

He only stared with wide eyes and an open mouth, completely at a loss for words. Perplexed by what the republic he had fought for, for so long, had become.

After the senators were well on their way, he led the way towards the exit. I leaned in closer to hear his orders over the distant—but still booming—roar. But he still said nothing.

As we exited out into the cold morning air, I watched as the senators, with Nasica at their helm, formed a wedge of sorts and pushed through the crowds of people.

They parted around him as if he had leprosy, for as Nasica once said, no man can touch a pontifex maximus and live.

While I was still transfixed, Scipio broke into a sprint

towards the mob. I didn't know what he was doing, and I don't believe he did either.

Tiberius and his loyalists were then held up at the temple of Jupiter Capitolinus, directly north of the temple which we were departing. From the looks of it, there were some 3,000 standing in defense of the tribune, but these too parted at the sight of the high priest.

I shot off like a bolt of Jupiter's lightning in pursuit of my general, and I was close enough to see Nasica lift his purple robes over his head.

And I've always wondered what that meant.

Was he showing the people his robes in trust that they would see his rank and position and part for him? Or was it more sinister? Was he signaling that he was about to make a noble sacrifice of Tiberius?

I presume I'll never know for certain.

When the crowds broke directly to where the tribune now stood, unarmed, Scipio stopped. I believe all of Rome did, save Nasica and his followers.

Tiberius was covered in blood. It appeared to be his own. His hair was disheveled and his toga was ripped and no longer poised around his hips and forearm in such a fashionable way.

His little brother Gaius was behind him. My old comrade from the legion stood confidently beside his older brother, but the tribune turned to him and shook his head.

"Run!" He shouted.

Nasica inched closer, his left hand clutching those purple robes over his head.

Tiberius stood his ground. He bounced backwards a bit, tentatively, but was careful not to run. Tiberius was willing to sacrifice anything but his dignitas.

The supporters around him ran away from the pontifex maximus so fast that they were tripping over themselves.

Even the most loyal of Tiberius' followers stood frozen in the high priest's glare, unable to strike. Nor did Tiberius ask them to.

"Brother," I heard my general say, his voice barely audible.

The tribune's eyes were wild, like a wounded animal. He seemed to inhale rapidly, without ever exhaling.

But he did not run.

Nasica approached. Slowly, he pulled the purple robes from his head.

He plunged a dagger into the tribune's belly.

Tiberius' body twitched at the blade, but he did not cry out. As many dying men do, he fell into the embrace.

He writhed, silently, and placed his head on Nasica's shoulder. As the blood began to trickle through his teeth and over his lips, I still believe he was looking directly at Aemilianus.

The whole world became still. Tiberius' supporters, who had been running away like rabbits, froze. The senators did too. The massive, towering statue of Jupiter watched placidly, but there was sadness in his eyes.

Scipio's jaw wavered like he wanted to shout something out, but he could not.

After the silence and stillness had seemed to stretch out for a life-age, the other senators surrounded the tribune. With their makeshift clubs, they beat him, one by one. His eyes remained fixed onto Scipio until he collapsed beneath them.

THERE WAS a pilgrimage made to the River Tiber the following day. For this was to be the final resting place of Tiberius Gracchus. His brother Gaius had pleaded incessantly with the nobles to allow him to bury his brother properly that evening. He was denied.

Nasica had Tiberius' remains, along with all those who had fallen in his defense, gathered and tossed into the Tiber. The following day, both those who hated and loved Tiberius came to gaze at the corpses where they had collected along the riverbank.

Shopkeepers stationed themselves nearby to offer meat or wine at a discounted rate for the mourners. The tribune-elects stood nearby, partitioned to various areas along the bank, shaking the hands of the passersby, letting them know that when the elections were rescheduled, they were the man to vote for.

Scipio wore his thickest winter shawl. He had a strong constitution and never seemed bothered by the cold, but he wrapped up in a bundle that day.

His rank allowed him to skip the lines. People moaned as we passed them by, as they were ready to gaze upon the spectacle of Tiberius' tattered corpse as if he were a chariot race or an Etruscan work of art.

I followed my general in close order.

But I had no desire to see Tiberius' remains. The more bruised and beaten he was, the more I would desire to do something which would end my career, if not get me executed in the process.

But when we arrived, I could not look away. Somehow, he appeared the same as I remembered him. Bobbing in the water, pall as a shade of hades, his mouth and eyes both open, as if he were still seeing a bright future or wished to speak. He was just as noble and charismatic in death as he was in life. Even his worst enemy, even Nasica, could not take that way from him.

He moved with the ebb and flow of the water, bobbing up against the riverbank, weeds already tangling with his hair.

Aemilianus was having trouble breathing beside me. Only I was close enough to see the tears in his eyes. He stifled his weeping and wiped the tears, as I dried my own.

"May all who do such things so perish," he said, quoting Homer. But the pain my general felt was real.

He turned and tried to walk, but stumbled. I caught him and bore his weight as we left.

And there I saw Gaius Gracchus and his mother. She was crouched, warm tears streaming down her face.

And he stood, frozen like a statue as his brother once was, with the most profound emptiness a man can imagine. His gaze was locked with his dead brother's. There were several streaks through the dirt dried on his face. And in those eyes I saw something that pained and terrified me. Where there was supposed to be white, I saw red. And I believe he was seeing red too.

I had known him as a playful young boy. The kind who so recently fed grapes and dates to his lover while the men discussed politics. The kind of boy who believed in ideals like nobility but wanted only to be with his loved ones, share a nice meal, and discuss the finer things.

But I could see immediately that this naïve boy had died with his brother. Someone else had taken his place. And everything that was yet to come was explained by those eyes.

But that story requires its own account, which I hope to recollect for you some other time.

Consul Scaevola, who had refused to act against the revolutionary tribune, now refused to act against his murderers. Nasica was not held to account, and neither were the others. In fact, there were claims about who, as if it were a badge of honor, had struck the second or third or final blow.

All of Tiberius' legislation, except for the land redistribution, were immediately nullified. The lands of Attallus III were immediately given to the senate to redistribute how they pleased. The length of service was never shortened (well, until yours truly came to power).

During the following year, the first new building in several years, the Aqua Tepula, would begin construction. This helped alleviate the unemployment, at least temporarily.

There were drafts for wars in Illyria and Asia, but these didn't seem to strain the population as much as they had before Tiberius.

Mucius Scaevola's Co-Consul Calpurnius Piso immediately left for Sicily to put down the slave uprising in the hope that this would provide Rome's granaries with an increased grain dole.

The Republic seemed to move on without Tiberius, even though the effects of his efforts were seen everywhere. The people didn't clamor for the death of the perpetrators. After all, who could they rally behind, now that Tiberius was dead?

But none of this stopped Nasica from becoming the most hated man in Rome. The Senate, probably out of self-protection, sent their high priest away to Asia Minor, under the guise of "restructuring it". But anyone with an understanding of Roman politics knew how ridiculous that claim was.

A pontifex maximus was never permitted to leave Rome under normal circumstances.

But he had become a liability for them.

Nasica left as he was told. And within a few months, he was dead. Dead of "natural causes" they said, but we knew what that really meant.

None of this kept Tiberius enemies from tracking down his allies, those who were ipso facto guilty of crimes by their association with the revolutionary. Many of his friends and allies were executed. One was put into a drum with serpents and cast out into the sea. All of his childhood tutors were brought before the consuls for judgment.

All of them died but one. When they brought Blossius the Stoic, who Cornelia had purchased for her sons when Tiberius was just a boy, was brought before the consuls, he did not relent.

It was Gaius Laelius himself who asked, "If Tiberius had asked you to set fire to the capital, would you have done it?"

"Yes. If Tiberius had asked me to do that, I would have done it." The crowds massed were initially in upheaval. But Blossius continued. "If Tiberius would have asked such a thing, he would have asked it for the good of the Roman Republic."

Blossius was released. He was allowed to flee with his life, and he fled to Asia Minor. Within a few years he would commit suicide, during a fight to create a free state for King Aristonicus of Pergamum, after that king failed to reclaim his state from the Roman senate.

Scipio Aemilianus, for all his nobility, did all he could to maintain the image that he was neither shocked nor wounded by the death of Tiberius. I knew this was false of course, but the rest of the Republic seemed to believe it.

Within the next few years, he was brought before the assembly, and an ambitious young tribune asked him, before the people, whether he believed it was just that Tiberius was murdered. He attempted for a long time to neither confirm nor deny the claim, but when pushed said, "of course it was just for him to be murdered, *if* it was his claim to take the Republic for his own."

He said it as tactfully as any man could, but it didn't matter. Rome's conquering hero became her pariah.

Tiberius' little brother Gaius, as well as several other tribunes, would go on to debate Scipio Aemilianus from the rostra. And here they would defeat him. His name was slandered in such a way that it made it nearly impossible to imagine Scipio could reclaim his status as Rome's hero.

The night of the debate, he would rest in his bed, the one I had sat beside so many times, with a tablet. He wanted to write a speech to explain himself... perhaps to say that he missed the revolutionary tribune as much as anyone, and he regretted that it was necessary that he should die. Perhaps he wanted to say that he had nothing to do with Tiberius' murder or had even tried to prevent it.

But it didn't matter.

The next morning Sempronia tried to shake him awake. But he was dead. In the prime of the general's life, he failed to rise from his slumber. Some say to this day that Gaius Gracchus was the one who did it. They say he paid someone to smother Scipio Aemilianus in his sleep.

Even in my old age, I've never believed it. And if I had, I would surely have sought vengeance. Gaius was no doubt capable and willing to do such a thing, but I've always believed Scipio died of the heartache and old age which descended on him quickly after his brother by law was murdered. The Republic he fought for simply wasn't the one he returned to.

And thus passed the age of Tiberius Gracchus.

Up until that moment in time, every dispute between the people and the senate had been peacefully resolved. The two sides made concessions: the senate out of fear of the people, the people out of respect for the senate. But this dispute resolved only with the blood of Romans. And a lot of them.

The senate said that only one man needed to die, and then Rome could return to the way she had always been. But I'm not so sure.

I hope the days of civil strife are behind us. But I sense something in the air that reminds me of that time.

We shall see.

Prepare yourself, Sertorius.

Be sure to <u>JOIN THE LEGION!</u> You'll receive family trees, high-res maps, a glossary, and other companion materials for your reading of Vincent's books! On top of that, you'll receive other novellas like this for FREE in the future!

ACKNOWLEDGMENTS

I have to first thank Conor Franklin for listening to this entire story, scene by scene, as I wrote them. He was the first to shake his head in derision when I wrote something poorly, and the first to clap his hands when I wrote something well. Conor, this story would have looked quite different (and for the worst, I believe) had it not been for your input. I believe by the end of my first draft you were as passionate about "The People's Tribune" and this tale as I was. Because of your feedback and additions, I believe many of my readers will as well.

I must also thank Leah Shaver and Michael Ager for the incredible work they did in polishing this book, helping me consider better alternatives to word choice, etc. Without these two this book would certainly be rougher around the edges than it currently is.

Finally, I'd like to thank "The Legion", my loyal subscribers who have been so incredibly supportive and patient with me as I've been writing the second book in The Marius Scrolls. I'm convinced you are the best readers in the world, and I cannot possibly explain how much your support means to me. I hope to continue providing you all with the best stories I know how.

Printed in Great Britain
by Amazon

25467485R00071